THE MAGICAL BOOKSHOP: 6

Fully BOOKED

LIZ HEDGECOCK

WHITE
RHINO
BOOKS

Copyright © Liz Hedgecock, 2022

All rights reserved. Apart from any use permitted under UK copyright law, no part of this publication may be reproduced, stored in a retrieval system, or transmitted, in any form or by any means, electronic, mechanical, photocopying, recording or otherwise, without the prior written permission of the copyright owner.

This is a work of fiction. Names, characters, businesses, places, events and incidents are either the products of the author's imagination or used in a fictitious manner. Any resemblance to actual persons, living or dead, or actual events is purely coincidental.

ISBN-13: 979-8423450830

*For libraries and bookshops everywhere,
and those who work in them.
As Jasper says, people make a library.*

Chapter 1

Jemma strode down Charing Cross Road, looking neither left nor right. No bookshop window or cake display would divert her from her course.

She had thought of taking a taxi, then decided to walk. *Walking means exercise and fresh air: two things I haven't managed much of lately.*

'Jemma, at least have lunch before you go,' Maddy had said, her brow furrowed with worry. 'You've barely stopped this week. Or this month. Or last month, come to that.'

'I've had breaks,' said Jemma. 'We had a tea break this morning, remember?'

'Which you spent staring at your phone,' said Maddy. 'I know it's an . . . interesting time, but there's no point working yourself into the ground. You have to relax sometimes.'

'I'll relax when the danger's over,' Jemma retorted, picking up her bag. 'Now I'm going to take a leisurely stroll to the London Library and try to surprise Jasper

Bantam.'

Maddy rolled her eyes, and said nothing.

I'll have a hot bath later, thought Jemma, as she hurried along. *I'll cook something. Yes, I'll cook a risotto.* Lots of stirring. Slow, slow, stirring. *I should video myself stirring and send it to Maddy.* She snorted, then visualised herself beavering away at a risotto for one, and sighed. Cooking was less fun without Carl there to appreciate it. He was somewhere in East Anglia, possibly Great Yarmouth, continuing his achingly slow circumnavigation of the country with his play.

Muffled ringing came from her bag and she tensed. It was the ringtone she had assigned to everyone on her British Library patrol rota. In this instance, the display said *Hermione*. She punched at the answer button. 'Hello?'

'Don't worry, Jemma,' said Hermione. 'I'm ringing with the all-clear.'

Jemma glanced at the time and exhaled. 'Of course you are. Yes. Anything to report?'

'Nothing whatsoever,' said Hermione. 'Nice and quiet. No sign of Drusilla, or any jiggery-pokery. I've handed over to Phil and grabbed lunch, and I'm heading for the Tube.' A pause. 'How are things with you?'

'Oh, you know. Busy.'

'Yes, I imagine they are.' Jemma heard a dog barking in the background. 'How long will we keep standing guard? It's been, what, a month? Six weeks?'

Jemma shrugged, then realised Hermione couldn't see. 'As long as it takes,' she said. 'I'm doing my best, I really am, but getting information is much harder than you think.'

Hermione laughed. 'I'm a librarian, remember? I spend my life looking for things.' She sighed. 'I wish we could find Drusilla. It makes no sense that she would cause so much trouble, then vanish into thin air.' She paused, but Jemma had nothing to add. 'Better go, I'm at the Tube.' Jemma was about to end the call when Hermione spoke again. 'Maybe we could meet for coffee some time, like normal people.'

'Yes. We should,' said Jemma. 'I'll let you go. Thanks, Hermione.'

'No problem. Bye.'

'Bye.' Jemma ended the call and checked her phone. More messages had arrived:

Jemma, do I need any special equipment? I'm bringing a knowledge emergency kit, of course, but should I wear a boiler suit?

Hi Jemma, can I swap my shift at the BL? Someone's put a meeting in my diary and I can't get out of it. My best times are Thursday morning and Monday afternoon.

Hi Jemma, what's the protocol for reporting unrelated incidents? Someone stole a pencil in the gift shop. I wasn't sure what to do, so I let it go, but do we have a procedure?

Jemma locked her phone, dropped it into her bag, and continued to power-walk to the London Library.

***

Jemma gazed at the tall, imposing building. *Once I was scared to go in*, she thought. She still was, but for a different reason. She sighed, found her membership card, and opened the door.

The woman at reception greeted her with a beaming smile. 'That's what we like to see, people who have their card ready. Now, are you aware of the rules of the library?'

'I am, yes,' said Jemma.

'You'll need to put your bag in a locker—'

'Could I speak to Jasper Bantam?'

'I'll see if he's in. Does he know you're coming?'

'Um, no, I just popped in on the off-chance.'

The receptionist reached for the phone on her desk. 'Can you give me your name, please.'

'Jemma James. He's sort of a friend.'

The receptionist gazed into space as she listened to the phone. 'Good afternoon, I've got a Jemma James here who would like to speak with Jasper.' She listened for a few moments. 'I'll inform her. Thank you.' She put the phone down and looked at Jemma. 'I'm sorry, he isn't available at present.'

'Oh. When will he be free?'

'I'm afraid he's tied up all day. Is there anything else I can do for you?'

The word *no* was on Jemma's lips when she had a sudden thought. 'Yes. I'll visit the reading room.' *I may as well, or this trip has been for nothing.* Her bag safely deposited, she made her way upstairs.

After several failed attempts, Jemma had finally managed to get more information out of Lennox Nash, her temporary boss, about the knowledge emergency he had attended at the library, including where it had taken place. She climbed the pink-carpeted stairs, enjoying the feel of the smooth banister under her hand, and entered the reading room.

The last time she had visited, it had been in the throes of a Grade One knowledge emergency, its readers flattened against the wall in terror. Now, though, it seemed exactly as it should: calm and quiet. A sprinkling of readers, heads bent, paged carefully through volumes and wrote in notebooks. A few looked up at her entrance with vaguely censorious expressions which said *I hope you're here for a good reason.*

Jemma moved between the desks until she reached the steps to the walkway where everything had happened when she had visited. Now they were firm and steady, the handrail cool, the books solidly planted on the shelves as they ought to be. She descended and approached a trolley, breathing as deeply and regularly as she could manage. A few books lay on the trolley. She picked up a couple; they came easily, not pulling other books with them. She shrugged, put them down, and walked to the door.

Before she left, Jemma surveyed the room. *After all,* she thought as she took in the detail, *I've only ever seen the library in turmoil.* But even the most detailed scrutiny revealed nothing of concern. *You're trying to make something of nothing, Jemma.* Then she caught sight of the clock on the wall. *You'd better get moving, or you'll be late meeting Lennox.* That gave her feet wings, and five minutes later she had reclaimed her bag and was hurrying to Burns Books.

***

As she sped along Jemma tried not to let her mind dwell on the mysterious disappearance of Jasper Bantam.

It's been going on for weeks, anyway. He probably doesn't want to get entangled with someone who has to be rescued. Although that's hardly my fault. I was only doing my job.

And he ought to be doing his, her annoying inner voice replied. *Not avoiding you when it comes to a professional matter.*

But he doesn't know that, Jemma argued.

He ought to. You've phoned him on the shop phone as well as your mobile. In a perfectly professional manner. She waited for the voice to add *So there*, but it didn't.

Jemma pumped her arms and walked extra fast to drive away the thought, to such good effect that she almost walked past the bookshop and had to do an abrupt about-turn.

'Getting some steps in?' asked Luke, with a grin. 'You need a sweatband and leg warmers.'

'Yeah, maybe,' said Jemma. 'Is Lennox in?'

'Ah,' said Luke. 'He rang a few minutes ago to say he might be a bit late.'

Jemma fixed him with a steely gaze. 'How late?'

Luke took a step back. 'Don't shoot the messenger. He said a bit. Actually, he said not more than five minutes.'

'Right,' said Jemma, knowing that could mean anything from ten minutes to half an hour. 'In that case, I'll get my lunch from the Friendly Bookshop and come back.' She focused on Luke. 'Sorry, how was your morning?'

'Oh, fine,' said Luke. 'Busy, obviously, as Em and I have been on our own.'

'Sorry. I'd have sent Maddy, but I was sorting next week's British Library rota and following up reported

Drusilla sightings.'

Luke's eyes widened. 'Anything?'

Jemma shook her head. 'Nothing conclusive. There are an awful lot of well-dressed blonde women in late middle age. Besides, she won't be walking around as herself, will she?'

'True.' Luke sighed. 'I wish I could see an end to it.' Then he saw Jemma's concerned expression. 'Anyway, go and get your lunch. At least hunger is easily fixed.'

Jemma dashed to the Friendly Bookshop, barrelled in calling 'I'm not stopping' to Maddy, and got her tuna sandwich and apple from the back room. 'Healthy eating,' she said to Luna, who was stretched out in her basket with two kittens feeding, while the other two chased a speck of fluff around the floor. 'And you're doing very well too.'

'Meow,' Luna replied, with a sleepy blink.

Jemma jogged to Burns Books and flung open the door to see the impeccably clad back view of Lennox Nash. 'Well, as she isn't here I'll pop out for lunch. I've just got time before my next meeting—'

'I am here,' said Jemma. 'Luke told me you'd be late, so I took the opportunity to fetch my lunch. And according to that clock, I'm exactly on time.'

'Mmm,' said Lennox. He consulted his own wrist. 'That clock's slow.' He narrowed his eyes at it and the minute hand moved forward until it touched the 1. 'Anyway, since you're here now, we'd better get on with it. Unless you'd rather eat your lunch, that is.' His sea-green gaze settled on the brown-paper bag Jemma was holding, and his long straight nose wrinkled a little.

'My lunch can wait, thank you,' Jemma replied, trying not to fume. After all the double bookings, the sorry-I'm-busys, the feeble excuses, she wasn't going to turn down the opportunity to examine the book which had made such a horrible mess in the British Library.

Lennox raised an eyebrow. 'Sure?'

'Sure,' said Jemma. 'We need to examine that book.'

He sighed. 'It isn't particularly convenient. I have another meeting at two o'clock, and if the book emits any . . . substances, I haven't time to get home and change.'

'I'll handle the book, then,' said Jemma.

Lennox surveyed the shop as if looking for a way out. Presumably, however, he found none, since he sighed again. 'Very well. Let's get this over with.'

Luke reached beneath the shop counter and held up two knowledge emergency kitbags, which Lennox took. 'After you, Jemma. As you're so keen.' And Jemma, feeling more or less equal proportions of resentment, excitement, and apprehension, led the way to the stockroom.

Chapter 2

Jemma turned the key in the lock, and the small metallic click it made did nothing to reassure her. It felt as if she had cocked a gun. *Show no fear,* Jemma told herself, and opened the stockroom door.

Everything was as usual: rows of shelves set out in aisles, mostly filled with cardboard boxes. There was no real point in labelling the boxes, since the books within tended to shift around according to the whim of the bookshop, or to reflect what stock was required at any particular time. However, dotted among the cardboard boxes were various smaller black boxes, many bound in silver chains, each designed to hold a single book. Those were a different story altogether.

'Where did you put it?' Jemma asked Lennox. Only then did she realise that the book – *that* book – could be anywhere in the room. *It could be over there. It could be behind me.* The hairs on the back of her neck prickled and she turned slowly in the space, trying to sense where it was.

'It's in the far corner,' said Lennox. 'As far from any other books as possible. I'll show you.' He took Jemma to the rear aisle and pointed at a box stowed on the top shelf. 'I didn't want anyone to take it out by accident.'

'Well, no.' Jemma fetched a step stool and retrieved the box. It was cool to the touch, and unreactive. 'I'll bring it to the table. We'd better suit up first.' She opened one of the knowledge emergency kitbags and took out a pair of goggles, a large handkerchief, which she tied over her nose and mouth, and a pair of leather gauntlets.

'Probably best to undo the padlock before you put those on,' Lennox pointed out, and Jemma swallowed a retort.

She examined the padlock and selected a silver key from her ring. In one movement, she opened the padlock and pulled the chain away. She took a step back, pulling on her gloves.

Lennox laughed. 'It won't bite.'

'I'm not taking any chances,' said Jemma. She opened the lid of the box, revealing another, chained box.

'*Now* you'd better be careful,' observed Lennox.

'Thank you so much.' Jemma peered at the padlock, and the box gave a sudden convulsive rattle which made her jump.

She stared at the box, trying to slow her breathing. 'OK,' she said, at last. She took her gloves off to search for a key, and having found it, put them back on. Behind her, she heard a tiny huff of breath. *I don't care if it takes me five minutes to get the box open; I'm not risking anything with this. I've seen what it did. He can huff all he wants; he isn't the one tackling this.* She pointed the key at the box, as if taking aim at it, then inserted it in the padlock and gave one quick turn, restraining the box with her other hand.

The box jerked. 'I don't like this,' she murmured.

'It's probably grumpy because you've woken it up,' said Lennox. 'I'm sure it'll calm down in a moment. Open the lid so that we can get a look at it.'

Jemma twisted round and stared at him. 'Are you sure about this?'

Lennox spread his gloved hands. 'We can't examine it without seeing it, can we?'

'I suppose.' Jemma turned to the box, which had stopped jerking and settled into a loud vibration. 'Here goes.' She pushed the button which held the box closed.

The lid flew up with a puff of black oily smoke which made Jemma want to cough. Her eyes stung, but she kept her gaze locked on the book, which was pushing its way out of the box. Instinctively, she grabbed it and forced it back down.

'It does seem excited,' said Lennox.

'What do I do?' asked Jemma. It was taking all her strength, even the magical strength which her membership of the Keepers' Guild gave her, to keep the book in her grasp.

'You examine it, of course.' Judging by Lennox's voice, he was enjoying the spectacle. 'The book's only cross because you're handling it roughly. How would you feel if someone pushed you around like that?'

Jemma relaxed her hold on the book and it made a lunge for Lennox. 'Why don't you have a go?'

'I shall in a minute,' said Lennox, and she could have sworn he was smiling beneath his handkerchief. 'I'm letting you practise first.'

Jemma peered at the tiny silver lettering on the spine of the small black book. The front cover was plain, which was why she had initially mistaken it for a notebook or a sketchbook when she had spotted it in the British Library. '*The Gentle Art of Destruction*,' she read aloud. 'That doesn't sound very—'

'What did you say?' Lennox wasn't smiling now, but leaning forward and peering at the book. 'Repeat what you just said. Repeat it exactly.'

'*The Gentle Art of Destruction*.' As if to confirm her words, a small plume of smoke issued from the top of the book spine. It was pure black, thick and heavy, and struggled free of the book as if sorry to leave it. The book jerked towards Lennox again. 'I take it you've heard of it.'

'Oh, I've heard of it,' said Lennox, 'but I thought it was long since gone. That, or it never existed.' Above the handkerchief his eyes were round and grave, and he seemed paler than normal.

'Should I open it?' Jemma's hand moved to the edge of the cover, and as she touched it the book flipped out of her hands and landed on the floor. Lennox stared at it, then her. 'It doesn't like me,' she said, shrugging.

'No,' said Lennox, 'it doesn't.' He bent and picked up the book, which lay in his hand like a small dead bird.

'Why is it behaving for you, and not for me?'

'Careful handling,' Lennox replied. His voice was calm but he was breathing rapidly, and his forehead glistened with sweat. He opened the book and flicked through a few pages. 'Jemma, we should put this book away. I've seen all I need to.'

'I haven't,' said Jemma. 'Not that I particularly want to look inside, but it's my job. Anyway, you've calmed it down.' She reached out a hand and the book pulled back. Or had Lennox done it? She couldn't tell.

'Did you move the book?' she asked, narrowing her eyes.

'Of course not,' Lennox snapped. 'Don't be ridiculous, Jemma. That's it; we've seen enough.'

'Should we tell Raphael?' asked Jemma. 'If a book has been found that no one even knew was real, I'm sure he'll be interested.'

'Don't worry, I'll let Raphael know. I'm speaking to him later, anyway.' He paused, scrutinising her. 'You may do the paperwork.'

'I thought you'd say that,' Jemma replied, but he didn't crack a smile. He was focusing on the book as he laid it carefully in the lead-lined box. 'Hang on,' she said, 'I should see if there's an author listed on the title page, for the paperwork.' She moved forward and took the cover gently between her gloved fingertips, but the moment she lifted it, the book crumbled into smoking grey ash with a little sigh.

She stared at Lennox, open-mouthed. 'What happened? Why did it do that?'

Lennox was looking at the place where the book had been, a peculiar expression on his face. Eventually, he raised his eyes to Jemma and shrugged. 'It didn't want you to learn its secrets.' Gently, almost reverently, he closed the lid of the box. 'Some books are like that. They only share their knowledge with a select few.'

'So you're one of the select few, and I'm not,' said Jemma, feeling very small.

'Well, I am a Keeper,' said Lennox, drawing himself up to his full height. 'You haven't been an Assistant Keeper for long. In fact, you aren't even an Assistant Keeper any more.'

'Oh,' said Jemma. 'Sorry.'

'No, I'm sorry,' said Lennox, in rather a patronising way. 'I shouldn't have asked you to examine it. It was beyond your capabilities.' He handed the box to Jemma. 'At least you've saved on paperwork.'

'Shouldn't we document it anyway?' Jemma looked at the box. 'What do I do with this?'

'The ashes go in the bin, and the box will need a good clean before it can be reused.'

'We're throwing it away?' Jemma frowned. 'That doesn't seem right.'

'It's no more use to anyone, is it?' Lennox untied the handkerchief and removed his gloves. 'I shall leave you to it. Things to do, you see.'

'You and everyone else,' murmured Jemma.

'I'm sorry, I didn't catch that.' Lennox leaned forward with an enquiring expression.

'You said you had a meeting at two,' said Jemma, 'but there's nothing in the shop diary.'

'No, there isn't,' said Lennox, 'because I arranged it on the fly this morning. I'm having a chat with that nice young man, Ben. You remember, we interviewed him for the Berkshire job.'

'Why would you want to talk to him?' Jemma demanded, before she could stop herself. She and Ben had not got on well during their brief encounter a few weeks previously.

'My new Assistant Keeper has got to come from somewhere,' said Lennox. 'I have no idea why you and Raphael were so against him; he has a lot of potential. He's already completed an Assistant Keeper application form, too, which reduces the red tape.'

'I see,' said Jemma. 'I could find the job description and person spec for the role, if you like.'

'All in hand, Jemma,' Lennox replied. 'In any case, I wouldn't dream of asking. You aren't Assistant Keeper any more, for one thing, and you're so busy, aren't you? You and everyone else.' He rubbed his hands together briskly. 'Now if you don't mind, duty calls.' He flung the stockroom door wide open and strode out.

Jemma gazed after him, rooted to the spot. *He's going to give Ben my job, and there's nothing I can do.* For a moment, she wished that she hadn't resigned from her position. Then she took a deep breath. *I have to stop Drusilla, and that's all there is to it.*

But can I do that? She looked at the box in her hand. *This book destroyed itself rather than let me open it. What else is closed to me that I don't even know about?* A wave of uncertainty flooded through her and she wobbled on her feet. *I stopped Drusilla before, but was that luck?*

To steady herself, she focused on the silver bracelet she

wore on her left wrist, and the two stones, purple and deep yellow, winked at her. *At least I have Raphael's gift to protect me.* She gave it a couple of turns for luck, then left the stockroom and locked the door. Any other mysteries within could stay there for now.

Chapter 3

Luke glanced up as Jemma entered the main shop, carrying the clean book box. 'How did it go?'

She handed him the box. 'Didn't Lennox say?'

He glanced inside, raised his eyebrows, then stowed it under the counter. 'No. He inspected himself on his phone, shot his cuffs, and strolled out. Oh yes, and he said, "Expect me when you see me."'

'So he won't be back until nearly closing time, then,' said Jemma.

'No surprises there. Anyway, stop changing the subject. What was the book?'

'Was is the right word. It disintegrated as soon as I tried to open it.'

Luke goggled at her. 'Really?'

'Yeah. It didn't mind Lennox handling it, but it didn't want me to go anywhere near it. Lennox said I wasn't senior enough.' She sighed. 'I managed to read the title. *The Gentle Art of Destruction.*'

Luke whistled. 'That doesn't sound good.'

'No, and Lennox looked pretty serious.'

The bell jangled and Mohammed, one of their regular customers, came in. 'Shall I go downstairs and help out?' asked Jemma. 'Maddy won't mind.'

'That would be great, if you can,' said Luke. 'I've been pretty much tied to the till, and I've no idea how the stock is looking.' He eyed Mohammed. 'Maybe we can talk later,' he added, in a low voice.

'Maybe.' Jemma wasn't entirely sure she wanted to. *I destroyed a book*, she thought, as she walked downstairs. *I destroyed a book through incompetence.* She had half hoped Luke would say that of course the book hadn't destroyed itself because she was junior, that obviously wasn't it, and there must be another reason. But he hadn't. *A bit of fetching and carrying will help you feel better*, she told herself as she opened the great oak door. *At least you can't mess that up.*

As usual, the large lower floor of the bookshop was busier than upstairs. Some customers sat in armchairs, leafing through books, while others stood in silent contemplation of the shelves.

Mohammed turned to her. 'Would I like this?' he asked, holding out a copy of *The God of Small Things* for inspection.

'Um, I'm not sure; I haven't read it,' said Jemma.

His face fell. Then he addressed the shop in general. 'Has anyone read *The God of Small Things*?'

'I have,' said a woman in a red raincoat and knee-high boots.

'Me too,' said a young man in a beanie hat. They

moved towards Mohammed, who beamed.

Maybe we could start a book club, thought Jemma. *Once a month, or maybe even twice, on a weekday evening.*

Yes, because you haven't enough to do, said her annoying inner voice. *If anything, you should catch up on your own reading. You've had the same book on your bedside table for three weeks. Anyway, your job is to sell books, and you can't sell books that aren't on the shelves. Look at the place.*

Jemma gazed about her. It was true that many of the bookshelves, particularly in general fiction, were showing large gaps. She waved to Em, who was busy serving behind the café counter, then went upstairs and re-entered the stockroom, taking the small wheeled trolley from its place by the wall.

She had loaded three boxes on before she thought of her experience with Lennox not half an hour ago. She paused, then went to look at the gap where the book had been. *How can I reconcile running a bookshop and preventing book emergencies?*

Maybe you can't. And when the new Assistant Keeper is in post, you won't have to. Maddy can run the Friendly Bookshop while you deal with more important stuff.

If I can. She took a step towards the gap on the shelf, then shook herself, went to the trolley, and loaded two more boxes. She hummed to herself in the lift, mostly to stop the little voice from chipping in further, then wheeled the boxes to the counter and took the scissors from the drawer.

The first book out was *Neverwhere*, followed by a London travel guide, then a thriller called *Upheaval*. 'That isn't what I meant,' Jemma told the box.

Her mobile rang. She was tempted to ignore it, but it was the library rota ringtone. She sighed. 'Hello?'

'Hello, is that Jemma?' said a breathy voice.

'Yes, speaking.'

'It's Violet, from Marylebone. I agreed to do the evening shift at the British Library tonight, but, um, something's come up.'

'Oh.' *I bet it has.* When Jemma had put out a call for volunteers, Violet had sent an email filled with qualifiers such as *If you're absolutely desperate* and *I suppose I could,* but had declared her determination to *do my bit and pitch in for the greater good.* Tonight would have been her first shift. Except that now it wasn't. 'Don't worry, Violet, I'll cover it.'

'Oh, thank you.' She sounded very relieved. 'Of course, if you need anyone in the future—'

'I'll keep you in mind.' *No I won't. The last thing I need is someone who flakes at the last minute.* 'Got to go, Violet, bye.' She ended the call and put her phone on the counter with a clack.

'Can I pay, please?' A customer was standing in front of her with what looked like a full set of the Parasol Protectorate series.

'Yes, of course.' Jemma cleared a space on the counter for the books. 'Cash or card?'

Seeing a till open, more customers formed a queue, and before Jemma knew it an hour had passed with no books making it to the shelves. 'This till is closing in ten minutes,' she called. 'Otherwise there'll be no books left for you to buy.' A good-humoured groan rose around her. 'There's a till upstairs, you know,' she said, as she rang up more books.

The last customer served, she wheeled the trolley to the bookshelves and began to fill the gaps. 'We need general fiction,' she muttered to herself as book after book went back in the box, to be taken upstairs to travel or history or engineering. 'Thank you,' she said aloud, shelving *Railsea*, *Kraken*, and *The City and the City*. She studied the tentacles on the cover of *Kraken*. *Must try that some time.*

She packed the leftover books into two boxes and took them upstairs, exchanging them for another five boxes from the stockroom. This time she managed to get most of them on the fiction shelves. She sighed with pleasure at a job well done, then looked at the time. *How did it get to be half past three? I swear time works differently in here.* She stood up and texted Maddy. *Sorry, busy at BB. Lennox off on another jolly disguised as a meeting. Back in a few mins.* Then she walked over to the café, where Em was, for a wonder, not serving a customer but rearranging her depleted supply of cakes. 'I'm here to say hi and bye,' said Jemma, with a lopsided smile. 'You know how it is.'

'Yep,' said Em. 'Good job I like making coffee and chatting to customers.' She grinned. 'Shame Luke's upstairs so much at the moment, though.'

'It isn't as if he has a choice,' said Jemma. 'Hopefully, when the new Assistant Keeper comes, he can rejoin you.' She scrutinised Em. 'I didn't know you two were particularly friendly.'

'When you're constantly fire-fighting one crisis or another, you find out who you can depend on,' Em replied. 'He's been teaching me stuff.'

Jemma's eyes narrowed. 'What sort of stuff?' *Don't tell me Em will start transforming into a bat as well. Or attacking pigeons in the dead of night.* Her gaze fell to Em's neck, which appeared undamaged.

Was she imagining things, or was Em blushing? 'We were chatting one day, and… You know that thing he does when he sort of, um, smoulders? Usually when he's looking at Maddy.'

Jemma sighed. 'Yes, I know the thing. Casting glamour, he calls it.'

'That's it. I was saying that I felt left out, what with you and Raphael and Lennox and Luke all doing magic, and he said he could teach me the basics of the glamour thing if I wanted.' She paused. 'Actually, he said I was already doing some of it.'

'Right.' *Watch out, London.* Em was attractive enough with her shiny hair and enviable figure, never mind additional glamour. 'Have you learnt much yet?'

'Not really.' Em tucked a strand of hair behind her ear and smiled into the middle distance. Jemma heard crockery smash, followed by a man's voice: 'Oh gosh, sorry.'

'Maybe save it for special occasions,' she said. 'Or emergencies.'

'Would you like a cappuccino to take away?' Em asked.

'Yes, absolutely. That's exactly the charm level I'm

looking for,' said Jemma, with a grin.

On the short journey to the Friendly Bookshop, her mobile rang yet again. *What is it this time? Is Violet back on the rota? Has Phil had to leave the library to rescue a cat or do an emergency stocktake?* Then she realised the ringtone was her normal one. *Not Carl, then. Or Jasper.*

She tutted at herself and pulled the phone from her bag. It wasn't a number she recognised. 'Hello?'

'Good afternoon, Jemma,' said a voice she knew but couldn't place. 'This is the Assistant Curator from Sir John Soane's Museum.'

'Oh, um, hello.' *What does she want?* Jemma had visited the Assistant Curator once, months ago, to borrow a book. *I did return it, didn't I?*

'I expect you're wondering why I am telephoning you. It's rather an irregular matter, and not about books, but I gather that your role has changed recently.'

'Oh?' Jemma stopped walking, and moved to a shop doorway to avoid being jostled.

'Yes. We museum people look out for each other, though not in the same way as Keepers do, and today I received news of an odd phenomenon at the London Mithraeum.'

'An odd phenomenon?'

'Yes. The Mithraeum is a reconstructed temple of Mithras, and a brief show with lights and recorded sound takes place amongst the ruins of the temple. Earlier today, one of the security guards reported that he'd heard chanting coming from downstairs when no show was scheduled. When he went to investigate he found the lights moving like searchlights, and he said the words were different from normal, too. However, as he doesn't speak Latin, he couldn't make it out. I wondered if it would be worth your while to pay the Mithraeum a visit when you finish work. It's open late tonight.'

Jemma rubbed the skin between her eyebrows. Suddenly she felt exhausted. 'I'm afraid I can't.' She recalled her conversation with Violet. 'I have to cover someone's shift until eight.'

'I see,' said the Assistant Curator, her voice neutral. 'Perhaps you could visit another time. Or I could pass on further details, if I obtain any.'

'Yes, please do that.' Jemma checked the time on her phone. 'I must go. Bye.'

'Goodbye, Jemma.' The call ended. *I hope she isn't angry with me, but I can't do any more than I'm doing. I simply can't.* She sighed, dropped the phone into her bag, and hurried on to the Friendly Bookshop, hoping her cappuccino hadn't gone cold.

Chapter 4

At half past four, Jemma repeated the locking-up instructions to Maddy, gave her the spare keys, and headed for Leicester Square. She glanced at the cinema, which was plastered with posters for the latest blockbuster. *If only,* she thought, and made for the Underground and the Piccadilly line. It was less busy than she had expected; perhaps she had actually beaten the rush. The train came two minutes later, and she swayed with it, clinging to a pole.

Maddy had looked – not disappointed exactly, but slightly harried when Jemma had returned to the Friendly Bookshop. 'I'm really sorry,' Jemma began.

'It's fine,' said Maddy. 'I just wasn't sure if you were all right. I considered ringing, then decided I was overthinking it.'

'Next time I'll make sure I text you,' said Jemma. 'I got caught up.' She sighed. 'Lennox has gone for a chat with someone about my job. Someone I don't like.'

'Oh,' said Maddy. 'Why not?'

'I've only met him once, but he was obnoxious. And yet Lennox seems sure he's the man for the job. I suspect he won't even bother interviewing anybody else.'

'At least you won't have to work with him,' said Maddy. 'Unlike Luke, Em, and me. Anyway, it's temporary. Raphael insisted, didn't he?'

'I suppose.'

Raphael had refused to accept Jemma's resignation. On the video call they had had shortly after Jemma had unmasked Drusilla in the British Library, he had insisted it was a temporary sabbatical, to be reviewed in three months' time.

'Does that mean you'll be back in three months?' Jemma had asked, hope stirring in her heart.

'I didn't say that,' said Raphael. 'Let's not be too hasty. I wouldn't want you or Lennox to do anything you might regret.'

The memory made a new thought occur to Jemma. 'Lennox is temporary too, really, isn't he?' she said to Maddy.

'Thank heavens,' Maddy replied. She still hadn't forgiven Lennox for his attempt to charm her when he first arrived at Burns Books. 'The sooner Raphael is back, the better. Have you heard any more from him?'

'Not for a while,' said Jemma. 'I must message him about—' She had been going to say 'about the book', but she couldn't face explaining it to Maddy. 'I have to leave early today; I'm doing the late shift at the British Library. We can close early, or if you want you can stay on and lock up.'

'I'll keep the shop open,' said Maddy. 'People do visit on Thursday evenings, and our takings aren't great this week.'

Something else to worry over. Jemma knew the takings were down, probably because she didn't have time to create new window displays, or write recommendation cards, or hand-sell books to the customers. There were too many other things to do. 'Thanks, Maddy, I appreciate it,' she said. 'Don't stay open beyond five thirty. You need a break too.'

'OK.' Maddy scrutinised Jemma, and Jemma's stomach chose that moment to let out a loud rumble. 'Did you actually eat your lunch?'

Jemma remembered the brown-paper bag which she had dumped in Burns Books on the way to the stockroom. 'I meant to—'

'You need to eat, Jemma.' Maddy gazed at her with big, serious eyes. 'How will you catch Drusilla if you're weak and hungry? Right, wait here. I'm going to fetch your sandwich and watch you eat it.'

Jemma sighed, sat down behind the counter, and sipped her cappuccino, which was lukewarm. Two minutes later Maddy was back, clutching the sandwich bag, along with a second bag which turned out to contain a cinnamon roll.

Jemma looked at her. 'You didn't have to do that.'

'You need to eat,' Maddy repeated. 'If I have to help with that, I will.'

Jemma was pushed forwards as the Tube train slowed. 'The next station is King's Cross St Pancras,' said the automated voice, and people moved to the doors.

Jemma tried to work out which side of the train would pull up to the platform, and as usual, got it wrong. She struggled onto the platform and began the long journey out of the station. She smiled at the tourists taking pictures of themselves at Platform 9 3/4, next to the luggage trolley embedded in the wall.

From the station it was a short walk to the British Library. Jemma had got into the habit of rushing for a first glimpse of the building, worried that in her absence something might have happened. But the library was as solid and uncompromising as ever, and its patrons as unhurried. Jemma let out a pent-up breath, and made for the entrance.

'Good evening,' said the security guard, opening her bag and glancing into it for form's sake, then handing it to her. 'I didn't expect to see you tonight.'

'I'm covering for someone,' said Jemma.

'What, again? Hope you're getting overtime.'

Jemma laughed. Phil was lurking near the gift shop, wearing a hat and a raincoat and looking incredibly furtive. If she hadn't known who he was, she would have been very suspicious of him. 'I'll raise it with my boss,' she said, and went to join Phil.

Phil peered around in a manner which seemed designed to attract attention, then bent to mutter in her ear. 'Nothing to report.'

'Oh, good,' said Jemma, though her heart sank a little. *How long can we keep doing this?*

'May I stand down?' asked Phil. 'Or do you have matters to attend to before you commence surveillance?'

'No, I'm fine,' said Jemma.

'Good stuff. In that case I might, um, use the facilities. Back in a mo.' He scurried towards the toilets.

A man talking on his phone left one of the benches in the foyer and Jemma took his place. *I'm here for three hours; I may as well get comfortable.*

Phil returned a few minutes later, looking considerably more at ease with himself. 'I thought Violet was on tonight,' he observed.

'Something came up,' Jemma replied.

'Oh. Nothing serious, I hope.'

'I don't think so.'

He brightened. 'Jolly good. Glad you were able to step in. I mean, I could have managed, but it would have been sticky. Booked a restaurant tonight: wedding anniversary.'

'Oh, congratulations.' Jemma frowned as something nagged at her. *Dinner... Well, risotto's out of the question. I'm not messing about stirring things after three hours stuck here...* 'Oh, heck.'

'What is it?' Phil asked, eyebrows halfway up his forehead.

'Oh, nothing. I usually have a video chat with someone on Thursdays, that's all.'

Thursday Night Dinner, they called it. When Carl had visited a few weeks ago, they had resolved to spend more time together virtually, since they couldn't do it in real life.

'We could have dinner together on Thursdays, before the show,' said Carl. 'We could FaceTime, or Zoom, and chat while we eat. I could even cook.' So far Jemma had watched him consume a Pot Noodle, a cheese toastie, and a quarter-pounder burger with fries, but it was nice to unwind with him at the end of the day. To have something to look forward to; something in her diary that wasn't work.

'I'm sure you can reschedule,' said Phil. 'Must dash.' He gave her a conspiratorial smile. 'Good luck, Jemma.'

'Um, thanks.' Phil was already striding off, swinging his briefcase as he went.

Jemma sighed and settled on her bench. Normally she would have jumped at the chance to spend three hours exploring the British Library: roaming through the galleries and people watching in the café or the reading rooms. However, her duty was to stay near the entrance and detect any suspicious activity: a delivery from River Logistics, or the arrival of someone who, for no apparent reason, turned her stomach. Drusilla had appeared as a redheaded student before; she could be anyone.

For now, though, everything seemed normal.

Jemma took out her phone: *Sorry but I can't make it for dinner tonight,* she texted. *Someone pulled out of library cover so I had to step in. Love you x* She pressed *Send*, and waited.

A reply came a couple of minutes later. *I don't believe it. I was actually going to cook proper food. With a recipe!*

She grinned. *Go on, what is it?*

Cheesy pasta.

Do you need a recipe for cheesy pasta?

Yeah, if you want to get it just right. She imagined him sitting in the kitchen of whatever theatre they were playing tonight. She was prepared to bet there wouldn't be a cheese grater.

I bow to your superior knowledge ;-) Send me a picture x

You better believe it. Maybe we can do Sunday instead?

That would be nice. Better go, you're distracting me x

Haha catch you later x

Jemma put her phone in her bag and surveyed the foyer guiltily. *I did look up between messages. No one would expect me to sit for three hours staring at the door.* She yawned, then interlaced her fingers and stretched, gazing at the ceiling.

As she did so, the back of her neck prickled. Not much – certainly not enough to suggest that Drusilla was nearby – but enough to make her wary. She scanned the foyer for the dark-turquoise uniform of a River Logistics courier, but failed to see one. *What is it?*

It was coming from the door. No, not quite. *Near* the door.

A man was talking to the security guard. She couldn't see his face because he was partially hidden by the guard, but he was casually dressed in a bomber jacket and jeans. Then the guard glanced at her, raised a hand, and turned to the man.

Don't stare, Jemma told herself. She took her phone from her bag, opened the camera, and moved her thumbs as if texting. After a few moments she zoomed in, and moved the phone so that she could see both men.

The guard seemed to be explaining something. Then he stepped back so that the other man's profile was in full view. He was in his thirties, maybe, with cropped dark hair.

He replied to the guard, and Jemma wished she could listen in too. Then he looked straight at her.

Sergeant Hawkins – the police officer who tried to interview me at the Maughan Library! What is he doing here? And why is he looking at me? Jemma had a distinct feeling that she didn't want to know the answer.

The sergeant turned back to the guard, leaned forward and said something more, then pulled up his hood and walked out.

Jemma waited until the guard was at leisure, then walked over. 'Is everything all right?'

'Oh yes,' said the guard. 'Plain-clothes copper came in. He said he'd had a report of someone matching your description who was behaving oddly in the library. The time he gave was well before you came in, though, and nothing unusual has happened, anyway. I told him you were in the library for a perfectly good reason and suggested he find a more reliable informant.' He chuckled. 'He didn't like that much.'

'Thanks,' said Jemma. 'Do you know him? Has he been round here before?'

The guard considered. 'Might have seen him. To be honest, most police officers look the same to me. Don't you worry. You're doing important work, and don't you forget it.'

Jemma returned to her bench, her mind full of questions. *Did someone tip Sergeant Hawkins off, or did he follow me? If someone did tip him off, was that to get me into trouble, or because they did see someone who's the image of me behaving strangely in the library?* She shivered, and pushed that last thought as far away as she could. That wasn't a road she wanted to go down: no, not at all.

She folded her arms and stared at the door. *Think of nice things. Cooking: maybe I should make that risotto. Or I could choose names for the kittens. Umm . . . James Bond. Donatello. Marmalade. Midnight.* But no matter how she tried to fill her mind with pleasant things, she kept returning to her conversation with the guard and picking at it, like a scab she couldn't leave alone.

Chapter 5

The minutes ticked by slowly. At six o'clock, Jemma's phone beeped and a photo of a plate of pasta flashed up, stuck together with something pale yellow, and with black specks on top which she presumed were pepper.

Yum yum, she replied. *It's better than what I'm eating*, she thought. *Which at the moment consists of humble pie.* As on every shift so far at the British Library, Drusilla was conspicuous by her absence.

As Jemma watched and waited, she got her notebook out, drew a grid, and kept a tally of the age and apparent status of the people entering the library. It was easy, since there weren't many of them. *Maybe I should do this at the bookshops*, she thought. *But I don't have time, and it isn't my job any more.* Though other people were all around her, she felt lonelier than ever.

Eventually the time crawled round to a quarter to eight, and staff went into the different rooms to give a fifteen-minute warning. One came over to her. 'Anything?' she asked.

Jemma shook her head.

'I suppose that's good.' She grinned. 'I thought it would be more exciting than this.'

'It's my job to make sure it doesn't get exciting,' Jemma replied. *How miserable do I sound?* She smiled at the woman to make up for her dour words.

Fifteen minutes later, she was on her way back to the Tube station. Back to the Piccadilly line, and another evening of making a quick meal and either staring at the television or searching the internet in a futile attempt to track down Drusilla. *I have to do something different*, she thought as she walked. *I absolutely must.* She felt her footsteps dragging.

The Maughan Library. She hadn't returned there – hadn't dared to – but perhaps at this time of night, if they were open… She pulled out her phone and checked. *24-hour access. If I get out at Holborn, it's a few minutes' walk. It's on the way home. And hopefully only a few staff are in, so there's less chance of meeting those librarians.* Her footsteps quickened till she was half running.

She fretted as the train filled slowly with passengers, then halted two minutes after leaving King's Cross St Pancras. *Come on*, she urged it. Eventually the train got going again, with no explanation, swallowing and disgorging people along the way, until it crawled into Holborn station. She jumped off the train and made for the escalator, phone ready to get through the barriers. She had typed the library's postcode into her maps app on the way there.

The building was sepulchral in the darkness, but

somehow she found it less scary than it had been in full daylight. *I don't have to stay long. Ten or fifteen minutes, for a chat.* She hurried across the courtyard and slipped into the library behind a student with their ID card at the ready.

'Hold up there, please,' said a man wearing a purple lanyard round his neck and a walkie-talkie clipped to his belt. 'Do you have your ID card?'

'I'm sorry, no,' said Jemma. She considered telling him she'd left it at home, but decided that honesty – at least, partial honesty – was the best policy. 'I'm not actually a student; I'm on my way home from work and I thought I'd pop in. I saw some videos on YouTube about the weird thing that happened here a few weeks back? I'm interested in paranormal stuff, you see.'

'Oh.' He looked her up and down with a slight frown, and Jemma was glad that she was reasonably smart that day. 'I wasn't in when it happened – day off – but I heard it was really creepy. Books flying everywhere, hitting people and breaking things. And smoke. My mate Tony said it was like the library was possessed.'

'Wow,' breathed Jemma. 'What happened afterwards? I believe they managed to stop it, but did it ever happen again?'

He paused to inspect the ID cards of a few students waiting patiently nearby, and waved them through. Then he leaned closer. 'Not officially,' he said. 'But there's a funny feeling about the place, if you know what I mean. Like it's thinking about doing something. Waiting for the right opportunity. Especially in the round room. I don't go in there often because it isn't part of my beat, but it's always chilly, and if you ever go in, there aren't many people. The atmosphere makes them do their business and get out.'

'Oh no!' said Jemma. 'What a shame. Will someone, um, do something?'

'What's to do?' He spread his hands wide. 'You're interested in paranormal stuff, so you tell me. Say some magic words? Sprinkle salt? Burn incense? Try suggesting that to the librarians.' He snorted. 'But they've got someone in on the QT.'

'Have they?' Jemma racked her brains for who it could be. Lennox had never mentioned any new contacts from the library. Then again, would he? She noticed her companion wore rather an odd expression, and adjusted her face into what she hoped was wide-eyed innocence. 'Have they brought in a paranormal investigator, like on TV? Or a white witch? That might work.'

He laughed. 'Now that I want to see. No, they've got a police officer in. Not just any police officer; apparently he's from a special squad. Not the Met, but City of London. You're in luck: here he is now.'

He straightened up and waved. Jemma's heart sank as she followed his gaze and found herself looking into the eyes of Sergeant Hawkins, who was still wearing his bomber jacket. As soon as he registered who she was, he made a beeline for her. 'I doubt he'll tell you anything about the investigation, though. Keeps his cards close to his chest, that one.'

Jemma consulted an imaginary watch. 'Good heavens, is that the time? I'd better go or I'll miss *Ghost*

Investigators.' She turned, but her way was blocked by a group of students carrying large textbooks and looking determined. She tried to get round them, but they were immovable.

'Any more flying books, Sergeant?' the man called, and laughed.

'Not tonight, Joseph,' Sergeant Hawkins replied, but his eyes were on Jemma. 'What a surprise to see you, Ms James. To what do we owe the pleasure?'

'I was just going,' gabbled Jemma.

Joseph's eyes narrowed. 'How come you know him?'

'Oh, we're old acquaintances,' said Sergeant Hawkins, keeping his dark beady eyes on Jemma as if she might vanish otherwise. 'In fact, I ran into this young woman earlier this evening, at a different library.'

'You said you was on your way back from work!' Joseph gave her a hurt look.

'I was! I mean, I am. I work in books. Anyway, must go. *Ghost Investigators*. Move along, please,' she told the students, who moved obediently to the side.

She heard Sergeant Hawkins call 'Wait a minute!', and broke into a run. She didn't stop until she was a good distance down a silent, deserted Chancery Lane. Then she slowed to a walk, surprised that the sergeant hadn't given chase. *He has my address and contact details, though; why would he bother? He can drop in when I least expect it.* She shivered, and power-walked until she was on a busy street, within sight of a station.

***

The next morning, Jemma didn't go downstairs to open

the Friendly Bookshop till five to nine. She had told Maddy as much the evening before, when she texted to let her know she was safely home.

The reply came quickly. *OK, but why are you so late home? Did something happen?*

No, I popped in somewhere on my way home. See you tomorrow.

What sort of somewhere?

Jemma sighed. *I'm tired. I'll tell you tomorrow.*

And now it was tomorrow, and she was dreading a conversation with Maddy. Not because Maddy would tell her off – any scolding Maddy administered was likely to be in sorrow rather than in anger – but because she'd had enough.

In the end, though, the opportunity didn't arise, as Maddy was making a first cup of tea in the kitchen when the shop phone rang.

Jemma answered it. 'Good morning, the Friendly Bookshop.'

'That's Jemma, isn't it?' said the voice of the Assistant Curator from Sir John Soane's Museum. 'Excellent. You did say I could call if I learnt any more about the business at the Mithraeum.'

Jemma covered the mouthpiece, and huffed. 'Yes, I did.'

'The security guard managed to get a recording of the chanting yesterday evening, and he sent it to me,' said the Assistant Curator. 'Normally it's just voices chattering, but this was an actual chant, over and over again.'

'What did they say?'

'*Londinium, cave*,' said the Assistant Curator. 'London, beware. There's something else, too. I don't know if you've visited the Mithraeum, but on the ground floor there is a display case full of different artefacts: pottery fragments, jewellery, arrowheads... They're usually in a fairly haphazard order, but yesterday night all the weapons were grouped together in the middle of the case.' She paused. 'I thought I should make you aware.'

'Do you have any idea what it means?' asked Jemma. She was strongly tempted to sit down, or lean on the counter, but Maddy was standing in the doorway with two mugs of tea.

'I wish I did,' said the Assistant Curator, 'but it doesn't sound good.'

'No, it doesn't,' said Jemma. 'I'll open the bookshop and do a handover with my assistant, then I'll get down there.'

'It isn't open until ten o'clock,' said the Assistant Curator. 'Yes, I agree that sooner rather than later is probably best. Thank you, Jemma. Please let me know what you discover.'

'I will,' said Jemma. 'Bye for now.' She laid the receiver gently on its cradle and Maddy brought her mug of tea, eyes enquiring.

'Yes,' said Jemma, 'more trouble.'

'I thought as much,' said Maddy. 'Drink your tea while it's hot, fill me in about this and whatever happened last night, then tell me what needs doing. Have you fed the cats?'

'Of course I have,' Jemma replied.

'Have you fed yourself?'

'Yes.'

'With a proper breakfast?'

'Slice of toast,' said Jemma. 'I woke late.' That was true; but it was also true that she had dreamt of being chased through London by Sergeant Hawkins for most of the night. Dodging in and out of stations, leaping on buses, always half a step ahead, but always within reach of his grasping hand. She had awoken shaking, nauseous and exhausted. Half the slice of toast had gone in the bin. She had only attempted it because she knew Maddy would ask her.

'What am I going to do with you?' said Maddy, but there was no force in the words. 'Could you eat a banana?'

Slowly, Jemma nodded.

'Right.' Maddy rummaged in her tote bag and handed Jemma a banana. 'Wherever you're going, take a taxi. You don't have time for the Tube, and you can put it on expenses.'

'OK. Thank you.' Jemma peeled the banana and took a small bite. 'I suppose you want me to tell you about the phone call.'

'And everything else.' Maddy sat down, and waved at Jemma to do the same.

Half an hour later, Maddy was fully briefed. 'OK, you can go now,' she said. 'You are taking a knowledge emergency kit, aren't you?'

'Yes, of course.' Jemma pulled one out from under the counter and began to check through it. 'Handkerchief, tongs, padlock and chain—'

The shop phone rang. 'I'll get that,' said Maddy, reaching around her. 'Good morning, the Friendly Bookshop.' She listened for a few moments then held the phone out to Jemma, her face neutral. 'It's Lennox, for you.'

Jemma made a face, put down the kitbag, and took the receiver. 'Good morning, Lennox.'

'Good morning, Jemma.' Lennox sounded cheery, avuncular, and full of himself: a combination Jemma particularly disliked. 'Could I trouble you to pop over to Burns Books? Shouldn't take long.'

Jemma rolled her eyes. 'Yes, but can I ask why? I was about to go on a site visit.'

'You'll find out when you get here,' said Lennox. 'See you in two minutes.' The line went dead and she replaced the handset. 'He wants me to go to Burns Books,' she said to Maddy. 'He says it won't take long.'

'In that case, I'm glad you've had breakfast,' said Maddy. 'Don't worry, I'll hold the fort. Hopefully he'll let you go when you tell him about the Mithraeum.'

'That depends on whether it's more important than whatever he's bursting to tell me,' said Jemma. She put the kitbag away and slung her own bag over her shoulder. 'I'll text you when I know more, if I'm not back soon.'

'Best of luck,' said Maddy.

Jemma found herself hurrying to Burns Books. *What can it be?* Lennox had sounded pleased – very pleased. Perhaps it was a book contract, or a visiting lectureship, or one of the other things he valued so highly which had nothing to do with the bookshop. She pushed open the door and went in.

'Ah, Jemma, there you are,' said Lennox. Luke was behind the counter, his face expressionless. 'Allow me to introduce your new Assistant Keeper!' He turned to the counter and drummed on it. 'Ta-da!'

Out of the back room stepped Ben, well dressed in a three-piece navy pinstripe suit with a burnt-orange silk tie. He also wore a smug smile. *He looks like a younger, smaller version of Lennox.* 'Thank you for the introduction, Lennox,' he said, and the smile broadened to a grin. 'Delighted to be working with you, Jemma. Though I should warn you that things are going to change around here.'

'Aren't they just,' said Lennox, and gave him a hearty pat on the shoulder. 'Aren't they just.'

Chapter 6

'That's my philosophy in a nutshell,' said Ben. 'Not to push the book onto the customer, but to draw the customer towards the book. What I've outlined today will work a treat.'

'Except that it requires a complete reorganisation of the bookshop,' said Luke. 'I can't say outright that your idea won't work, but I would comment firstly that our sales are already good, and secondly, our customers know where to find the books they want.'

'Ah, but are they *drawn* to the books?'

'Knowing where to find them is always a good start,' said Jemma.

She had kept quiet during most of Ben's speech about his goals for the shop – no, not just the shop, the future book empire – and for London as a whole, not to mention a lengthy explanation of his bookselling philosophy. The atmosphere in the shop was distinctly chilly, and that wasn't entirely the bookshop's fault.

'Why don't we try it?' said Lennox. 'Moving books

around can't take that long. Anyway.' He flourished a white shirt cuff as he consulted his watch. 'I have a meeting to go to. Ben, would you like to accompany me? That will keep us busy till lunchtime, and I know a nice little Italian place round the corner.'

'I'd be delighted,' said Ben. He drained the espresso cup he had been holding for the last ten minutes – his third, at least – and handed it to Jemma. 'Take care of that for me, would you?'

Jemma managed to hold in a retort. 'When do you think you'll return, Lennox?'

'Dr Nash,' Lennox corrected. 'I have another meeting at two on the other side of London, so there's no point coming back here.'

'Will Ben be returning? I can't stay in the shop all day. I have a site visit to do, in case you've forgotten.'

'I hadn't forgotten,' said Lennox. 'However, I don't believe you mentioned where you were going. Is it necessary that you go today?'

'Absolutely.'

'Is it a bookshop? A library?' His tone was light, but Jemma felt as if she were supine in the dentist's chair as he probed for signs of weakness or vulnerability.

'It's the London Mithraeum. The Assistant Curator at Sir John Soane's Museum says strange things are happening there, and it might be related to our – problem.'

'What problem?' asked Ben. 'And what does a museum have to do with it?'

'As ever, Ben has reached the heart of the issue in one swift move,' said Lennox. 'What does a museum have to do with us, as Keepers? Frankly, I don't see why the AC at Soane's can't deal with it herself.'

'The museums don't have a Guild like we do,' said Jemma. 'She contacted me because she thought I could help.'

'Ah,' said Lennox. 'Presumably, you also think you can help.'

Ben smirked, and Jemma glared at him. 'Yes, I do,' she said quietly. 'At any rate, I'm prepared to take it seriously.'

'I don't have time to discuss the finer points of the matter with you, Jemma,' said Lennox. 'Some of us have work to do.'

'Yes, we do,' said Jemma. 'So why don't you and Ben go to your meeting, then have lunch together.'

'Hmph,' said Lennox. 'Come along, Ben, I'll fill you in on the situation as we go.' He strode to the door.

Ben tapped the nearest bookshelf. 'These books won't reorganise themselves, Jemma. I suggest you crack on, instead of going on your little trip.'

He sauntered after Lennox, and it was all Jemma could do not to throw the espresso cup at his head.

'Is this our future?' Luke said gloomily, once they had gone. 'Those two swanning around the place and giving orders, when they're not taking long lunches and going out to what they call meetings?'

'I'd love to say no,' said Jemma. 'Unfortunately, I don't think I can.'

The shop bell jangled and the two Golden Age crime ladies appeared. 'Oh dear,' said one of them, when she saw Jemma. 'You do look miserable. I hope no one's been murdered.'

Jemma forced herself to smile. 'It isn't as bad as that.'

'Well, that's a relief,' said the other Golden Age crime lady, and they wandered to the lift together, chatting.

Jemma turned to Luke. 'I'll take this cup down to the café, then help you move these books.'

'No you won't,' said Luke. 'You've got a site visit.'

'But—'

'It's only Ben's half-baked idea. Anyway, he's not the boss of you. If I have time, maybe, but serving the customers is my priority.' The atmosphere thinned, as if the shop had let out a breath it was holding. 'Discovering what's going on at the Mithraeum is your priority, if you and the Assistant Curator think it is.' He raised his eyebrows. 'What is going on?'

Briefly, Jemma explained.

'In that case, I can't believe you're still here,' said Luke. 'Off you go. Don't worry about the cup, I'll deal with it.'

'Thanks,' said Jemma. 'Sometimes I think I'm just…'

Luke's eyebrows climbed higher. 'Just what?'

'Reading too much into things?' *Maybe the walk to the Tube will clear my head.*

She strolled down Charing Cross Road, past Trafalgar Square, keeping her eyes averted from the pigeons, and along Northumberland Avenue towards Embankment. The District and Circle line was quiet, and Jemma found a seat on a battered old train. It was only three stops to Mansion House station, and Jemma emerged into the daylight again feeling pleased. *Hopefully I can find out whatever there is to know and get back before anyone has a chance to miss me.*

A phone was ringing somewhere: an old-fashioned pealing. *Probably someone's mobile*, she thought, and waited for it to stop. But it didn't. She shrugged and consulted her phone, which said the London Mithraeum was down Cannon Street and round the next corner.

As she walked, the ringing grew louder. *Is anyone going to answer that?* She scrutinised the people around her, but nobody seemed concerned. Yet by the time she turned left off Cannon Street, she could hardly hear herself think.

'Excuse me,' said a young man holding a guidebook. 'Could you tell me the way to the...' He peered at the book. 'The London Mithraeum?' He said the words carefully.

'It's down here,' said Jemma. 'Sorry about the noise. London isn't normally this noisy.'

'Oh, I'm used to traffic,' he replied.

'I meant the ringing,' said Jemma.

He looked puzzled. 'The ringing?'

After a pause, Jemma said, 'Never mind. That's it, there.' She pointed to the sign.

'Thank you,' said the young man. Pulling a folded sheet of paper from his pocket, he entered the building. *Should I go in, too? This is what I came for...* But the relentless ringing made it impossible to concentrate. *If no one else is aware of it –* she eyed the people hurrying by, probably heading for Cannon Street station – *it's up to me to answer it. That must be a heck of a big telephone.*

She took a few steps past the Mithraeum, and the

ringing became even louder. It seemed to come from a church with a tall tower further down the road. *That's nothing like church bells.* The church was pale grey and no different from any other London church she had seen, except that a dome peeped from behind the tower as if playing a game with her.

The sign on the church said *St Stephen Walbrook*. It meant nothing to Jemma, but the noise was so great that she feared the church would collapse if she didn't do something. So she went in.

The interior was not what she had expected: light, airy, and luxurious in white and gold. Above her rose the interior of the dome, which appeared much bigger from the inside. But the telephone was still ringing.

Jemma put her hands over her ears to dull the noise. *If I don't have a headache after this...* She followed the sound to a small white plinth on which, in a glass case, sat an old-fashioned black telephone with a receiver and a dial. It wasn't that different from the shop phone at Burns Books. On the plinth was a sign which began:

THIS IS THE TELEPHONE
MANSION HOUSE 9000.

'How do I answer it?' Jemma said, aloud.

'Can I help you?' asked a friendly voice, and Jemma turned to see a man standing there. He wasn't in a clerical outfit, but he seemed to belong to the church.

'Um, the phone's ringing?' She did her best not to shout, but even so he winced.

He smiled. 'I doubt it. For one thing, it isn't plugged in.'

'But it *is* ringing.'

He grinned, and put his ear against the case. 'I really don't—' Then he frowned, and cupped his ear with his hand. 'Well. You're right, it *is* ringing.' He took his ear away, then pressed it to the case. 'Yes, it definitely is. I'll just— I'm not sure where the key is.' He hurried off.

Jemma stepped back, watching the phone. In a cartoon, it would have been rattling with the noise it made, but it was motionless. *He heard it too. I'm not imagining things.*

A few minutes later, the man returned with a ring of keys like a giant version of her padlock keys. 'It'll be on here,' he said. 'The phone gets checked every so often. It's the Samaritans' phone, you see: the first phone on the helpline.' As he spoke, he was sorting through the keys. 'Here we are.' He unlocked the case and removed the glass top. Jemma had to move away; the ringing was absolutely deafening. He picked up the receiver and listened. 'It's quite faint; I can't make out any words.'

'Could I try?' asked Jemma. 'The phone was ringing very loudly, for me.'

The man looked at her doubtfully, then shrugged. 'If you do make it out, tell me what it says.' He handed her the receiver, then leaned over to check the back of the phone. 'No, it definitely isn't plugged in.'

Jemma held the receiver to her ear. Her first thought was that it was like the sound of the sea in a shell. Then the whooshing resolved itself into whispering: many voices crossing each other until they blended into one.

'London Stone… The London Stone… The London Stone is gone… The Stone is gone.'

Chapter 7

'The London Stone is gone,' Jemma repeated, feeling as if she were in a dream.

'I beg your pardon?'

'That's what it's saying. The London Stone is gone. What's the London Stone? And where is it?'

'It's a block of stone, obviously; I can't remember what sort. As for where it is, it's usually set into a niche in Cannon Street, a stone's throw from here.' His mouth quirked up on one side. 'Not that I suggest you do throw it; it would be very heavy.' He leaned forward. 'Try asking where it is, or who's taken it.'

Jemma did as he suggested, but the voices separated and blurred, then faded into silence. 'It's gone,' she said. 'Well, whoever it was – or whoever they were – has gone.' She looked at the phone doubtfully. 'Is there any way to trace the call?'

'You could dial 1471.'

The dial ticked reassuringly as her finger turned it, but when the call connected she got a recorded message: *We do not have the number for this call. Thank you.* 'No number,' she said, and replaced the receiver. 'What does it mean? What is the London Stone? It can't just be a big rock.'

'It depends who you talk to,' said the man. 'Some people say that Brutus of Troy set the London Stone; others that it's the stone from which King Arthur pulled Excalibur, or that it was a Druidic altar. And there's a superstition that if the stone is removed or destroyed, then London will fall. I'm sure that's only a myth—'

'Do you know whereabouts in Cannon Street it is?' asked Jemma.

'I do. It's at number 111, round the corner.'

'Everything's round the corner,' said Jemma. 'I'm only here because I was going to the London Mithraeum and I heard your phone ringing.'

The man lifted the phone again and listened, then hung up. 'Very strange... Perhaps someone should inform the Lord Mayor; that's the official guardian of the stone...' He came out of his reverie. 'May I ask your name, please?'

Jemma wondered whether to invent one, then told herself she was being silly. 'I'm Jemma James,' she said. 'I run the Friendly Bookshop on Charing Cross Road. Here, I'll give you my card.' She scrabbled in her bag and presented him with one. 'I'd better go to Cannon Street and see if it's true.'

'Yes, please do.' The man looked troubled. 'People say the myths about the stone are old wives' tales, but if I wasn't on duty, I'd come with you.'

'If it has gone, it will be all over the internet by now.'

On impulse, she put out a hand, and he shook it. 'Thank you for your help.'

'No, thank *you*.' He managed to smile through his bewilderment.

Jemma shouldered her bag and made for the door. She turned to wave and saw the man still standing by the plinth, gazing at her as if he wasn't quite sure if she were real or not. *I'm real*, she told herself, digging her thumbnail into a fingertip to make sure. *It's everything else that's the problem.*

She half expected to see a crowd as she approached 111 Cannon Street, but the niche in the wall was clearly visible, its glass window obscured every so often by a hurrying pedestrian.

Finally, she got close enough to see properly. 'It's true,' she whispered. 'It's gone.' The niche was empty.

'Not again.' The words were said with some force, and Jemma twisted round with a sickening feeling that she already knew who was behind her.

She was right. Looming over her, his face a mixture of surprise and annoyance, was the bomber-jacketed figure of Sergeant Hawkins. 'Tell me why I shouldn't arrest you right now.'

Jemma scrambled to her feet. 'It's nothing to do with me,' she said. 'I heard it was gone, so I came to check.'

'Right.' He pulled out a notebook. 'How did you find out? Who told you?'

Jemma eyed him. 'This probably sounds weird, but the Samaritans' phone rang, and a voice – lots of voices – said the London Stone was gone.'

'Back up a minute,' said Sergeant Hawkins. 'The Samaritans' phone? The one at the church?'

'That's it: St Stephen Walbrook. I've just come from there.'

'What were you doing in a church at' – he checked his watch – 'ten to eleven? You work in a bookshop on Charing Cross Road.'

'I was in the area on business,' said Jemma. The thought of being interrogated by Sergeant Hawkins, of trying to be honest while concealing the existence of the Keepers' Guild, was more than she could cope with. She looked him in the eye. 'What are *you* doing here?'

'I'm a police officer,' said Sergeant Hawkins, glaring at her. 'A City of London police officer, doing my job in the City of London, which is where I'm meant to be. Unlike you.'

'You're not on duty, though,' said Jemma. 'Not in your bomber jacket.'

'You've never heard of a plain-clothes officer? Any more lip from you, Ms James, and I'll arrest you for wasting police time. And I *could* arrest you for lurking at the scene of a crime in a suspicious manner.' His eyebrows unknitted slightly. 'I suppose it's too much to hope that you saw anything relating to the theft of the stone.'

'I'm afraid not,' said Jemma. 'Like I said, I found out it was gone and I came here. You can ask the man I spoke to at the church. He opened the phone case and took the call.' Now she was glad she had given her real name.

'So he heard the message, too.'

'Um, not exactly. He said there was whispering but he

couldn't make it out. Maybe his hearing isn't very good.'

'Right.' Sergeant Hawkins stuck his hands in his pockets, then seemed to remember that he was on duty and took them out. 'Luckily for you, I have too much going on to cross-examine you just now. But I shall be in touch, and I expect you – *expect* you – to come to the station when you're told and answer any darn question that I ask, to the best of your ability.'

'Yes, Sergeant Hawkins,' mumbled Jemma.

'Good.' He huffed out a breath. 'Now if you don't mind, I've got people to contact, forensics to coordinate, and a new stone to sort out.'

Jemma stared at him. 'A new stone?'

Slowly, the corners of Sergeant Hawkins's mouth lifted. 'You don't think that's the real London Stone, do you? What do you take us for?' He unslung his rucksack and pulled out a police radio. 'Hawkins here. Report confirmed. Operation Easter Island is go. Repeat, Easter Island is go. Over.'

'Can I ask you something?' asked Jemma.

'Yeah, but I might not answer.' He sighed. 'Go on.'

'How did you find out that the stone had disappeared?'

He pursed his lips, seeming to weigh up whether to answer or not. 'I ought to tell you to mind your own business,' he said, 'but I got a phone call. Not to my work number, but my personal mobile. Just like yours, it was a load of whispering voices telling me the London Stone was gone. It makes sense for me to get that call because it's my job, though how they got hold of my mobile number I have no idea. Why you?' He studied Jemma until she fidgeted.

'I have a distinct feeling there's more to this than you're letting on. A lot more. But I've got a situation to contain.'

A middle-aged couple approached them. The man had a camera slung around his neck. 'Isn't this where the London Stone is?' he asked, in what sounded like a Texan drawl.

'That's right,' said Sergeant Hawkins. 'It's being cleaned at the moment, but it'll be back in a day or two. Conservation work.'

'Well, that's no good to us,' the woman snapped. 'We're flying home this evening.'

'My apologies, madam, I'm terribly sorry that our ancient monuments clash with your schedule.' He waited until they had departed, bristling, and pulled out his radio again. 'Hawkins again regarding Operation Easter Island. Bring an official-looking sign that says, quote, London Stone has been removed for conservation work. We apologise for the inconvenience, unquote. Over.' He put the radio away. 'Don't you have a bookshop to run? Apart from anything else, you're attracting attention.'

'I apologise for the inconvenience,' said Jemma, and marched off in what she hoped was the right direction for the station. *Dodged a bullet there*, she thought, as she stalked along.

What the heck will I do if he calls me in and cross-examines me? That, if it happened, would be far harder to dodge. She imagined question after question, poking and probing, and shivered. *If he does arrest me, I won't have to worry about the bookshop or Drusilla.* That brought scant comfort.

When she reached Embankment station, she made her way to Burns Books. As she had expected, there was no sign of Lennox or Ben. Luke, however, was busy with a long queue. 'All OK?' she asked.

He grinned. 'Far too busy to reorganise bookshelves. Did you get to the Mithraeum?'

'It's a long story,' she replied. 'Is *Parishes and Wards* still in the stockroom?'

'It is,' said Luke. 'A customer asked if we had a copy the other day.' He grimaced. 'I lied and told him we'd order one.'

'Good work,' said Jemma, and went through to the stockroom. *Parishes and Wards*, or to give it its full title, *Parishes and Wards of Greater London and the City*, was at the top of the first box she opened.

She turned to the index and riffled through the pages. Sergeant Hawkins was right – Cannon Street was in the City of London. 'I didn't know the city had a separate police force,' Jemma murmured. She retrieved her own notebook, and scribbled: *Research divisions of the City of London Police*. Then she returned to the book.

The church of St Stephen Walbrook, reasonably enough, was in the ward of Walbrook, while the Mithraeum, though metres away, was in a ward called Cordwainer; Walbrook, the street separating them, marked the boundary. Cannon Street, meanwhile, while also in the ward of Walbrook, was right on the boundary of three wards: Walbrook, Dowgate, and Candlewick.

Jemma chewed the end of her pen, then went into the main shop. 'Luke, when you researched the Maughan

Library, can you remember what you found out about its location?'

Luke's brow furrowed. 'Let me think… Chancery Lane, isn't it? It's in Farringdon Without, so it's in the City of London but outside the London Wall. And I seem to remember that it's right on the edge.'

A customer who had just arrived at the counter gave him a significant look. 'I do apologise,' said Luke. 'Oh yes, an excellent choice, madam.'

Jemma returned to the stockroom, made a note of what she had found, then searched for Chancery Lane. It was, as Luke had said, right on the edge of the city.

What does that mean? And why does it matter? She wrote herself another note and closed the notebook. It was time to return to her own shop and take over from Maddy, though Maddy would probably come to Burns Books and help Luke rather than have a proper lunch break. She sighed, left the stockroom, and began to walk back.

Lennox is no use, she thought. *I can't spill the beans to Sergeant Hawkins, and he probably can't help anyway.* She brushed her fringe out of her eyes, and the stones of her silver bracelet gleamed in the struggling sunshine. *Of course. Raphael.*

Chapter 8

As Jemma had predicted, Maddy departed for her lunch murmuring that she might see if Luke needed anything at Burns Books. She had taken to bringing her lunch with her in the mornings lately, too.

It's lucky we have the staff we do, Jemma thought. *I suspect some people would leave us to sink or swim.* She texted Raphael: *Do you have time for a quick chat?*

It took a couple of minutes for him to respond. *Yes, give me five minutes. Video call? I'll be on the phone.*

Jemma imagined him typing furtively. To be fair, when she had first met Raphael, she would never have believed him capable of using a smartphone. *Yes please*, she replied, and pulled her laptop from the drawer.

She heard a squeak, and one of the kittens – the black one – scampered into the shop. Unfortunately the kitten hadn't learned how to stop yet, and momentum carried her under a bookcase, where she squeaked until Jemma knelt and gently retrieved her. 'You're not supposed to be in here,' she said.

'Meep,' said the kitten, opening her blue eyes wide.

Jemma sighed. She had been worried about leaving the kittens on their own in her flat all day, even with their parents Luna and Folio to care for them, and had installed cat flaps on the route down to the shop. While the flaps were lockable at night, this did mean that at any moment customers and staff were in imminent danger of being tripped by a skittering kitten, or by Luna and Folio sauntering in and treating the place like home, which it was. They rarely ventured to Burns Books now. 'I'll just check on you lot,' Jemma said to the kitten, stroking her little head, 'and then you'll have to behave, because I'm talking to Uncle Raphael.'

The kitten purred and rubbed her head against Jemma's finger as they climbed the stairs. In the flat, Luna and Folio were on the windowsill, basking in the pale sunlight like a pair of black and ginger sphinxes, with three kittens tumbling between them: one orange, one tortoiseshell, and one black and white. Jemma checked and refilled their food and water bowls, then attempted to dole out exactly the same amount of fuss to each cat, though the black and white one would get in the way and butt her hand whenever she reached for anyone but him. 'I ought to call you Lennox,' she told him. 'Always wanting more than your share of anything going.'

Folio gave a sharp meow. 'It was a joke,' she told him. 'I'm going downstairs.'

She fetched her own lunch from the fridge and settled with her laptop at the shop counter. She would have to hope that no demanding customers came in.

Raphael answered her call on the second ring. He sprang into view in portrait mode, wearing a navy suit jacket and an open-necked cream shirt. She missed his bright bow ties. She peered at the background, which looked like maroon tiles. 'Where are you?'

'I'm in the bathroom,' said Raphael. 'Never mind that. What's up?'

'How do you know something's up?' Jemma studied herself in the small window at the bottom of the screen that showed her own face. *I don't look any different from usual. Do I?*

'You asked for a call. You never ask for a call unless something's up. Or rather, unless you feel something's up.'

'Anyone would agree that something's up.' Quickly, she filled him in on the call from the Assistant Curator at Soane's, her journey to the London Mithraeum and subsequent diversion to St Stephen Walbrook, and the disappearance of the London Stone. 'Apparently the stone that's gone is a fake, so it's not as serious as it could be, but it's still bad.'

'How do you know it's a fake?' Raphael's tone was light and his face almost expressionless, which to Jemma indicated that he was very interested in the answer.

'A police officer told me. He arrived at Cannon Street a minute after I did. He'd had a call, too, the same as mine. And what's really weird is that he's one of the police officers who was at the Maughan Library knowledge emergency.'

'Does he have a name?'

'Sergeant Hawkins, and he said he was from the City of

London police.'

'Let me make a note of that,' said Raphael. He drew a small notebook and a pencil from the inner pocket of his jacket and scribbled, then peered at the result. 'He is who he says he is, according to this Pencil of Truth.'

'Oh, he's definitely a police officer,' said Jemma. 'He has that look about him, that he'll pounce on you if you aren't careful.'

'I hope you *were* careful,' said Raphael, frowning.

'Of course,' said Jemma. 'I said as little as I could. I'm not going to lie, though. Anyway, shouldn't we work with the police on this? I mean, the theft of the London Stone, or what people think is the London Stone, is an actual crime. But I discovered another thing which might be useful. Lots of the places we've had serious trouble with are on the boundary of a ward in the City of London. They're all on the edge of something.'

'Don't step on the cracks,' said Raphael, and smiled, though there was no mirth in it. 'Seriously, Jemma, don't lose sight of Drusilla.'

'I'm not. But don't you think that's related? The Maughan Library is right on the edge of the City of London, and she was behind that.'

'What about the British Library, or the London Library, or Charing Cross Library?'

'That's different, because she wanted to join them together and control the area inside—'

'We can't be sure of that.' He sighed. 'Sorry to sound harsh, Jemma, but it's perfectly possible that someone – or something – is trying to distract you from your pursuit of

Drusilla. While you're chasing round London after things that, let's face it, have nothing to do with books, she could be up to anything.'

'If you know so much, why don't you come back and sort it out?' retorted Jemma. Immediately, she regretted her words. 'I'm sorry, Raphael, I'm finding things quite tough at the moment. Apart from anything else, Lennox has recruited to my job. And it's Ben.'

Raphael looked pained. '*That* Ben? Hold-my-coat Ben? Let-me-tell-you-my-thoughts Ben? In-my-experience Ben?'

'The same. Lennox unveiled him this morning and he immediately suggested we reorganise Burns Books.'

Raphael drew back a little. 'I hope you didn't. The shop wouldn't take well to that.'

At that moment the black and white kitten scrambled up beside Jemma, then jumped on the counter and walked deliberately across her laptop. 'Honestly,' said Jemma, lifting him off, but when she looked at the screen she was sporting a pig's snout, a polka-dot bow tie, and a pair of deelyboppers. 'Aargh!' She tried to switch off the effects, in vain.

Raphael laughed. 'The kittens are developing well, then.'

'They've got the worst traits of both their parents,' said Jemma.

The tortoiseshell kitten joined the first kitten on the counter and flopped down by the laptop, her paw hovering over the Delete button. 'No you don't,' Jemma said, moving her away.

'Have you named them yet?' asked Raphael.

'John, Paul, George, and Ringo. Flopsy, Mopsy, Cottontail and Peter.' Jemma sighed. 'I haven't had the headspace to choose names. At this rate they might end up as One, Two, Three, and Four.'

'Paper sizes? Quarto, Octavo, Foolscap, and . . . A4? Or something to do with the moon, like Luna?'

'I'll think of names soon, I promise.' Jemma tried to remember what they had been talking about before the kittens had sabotaged the conversation. 'Anyway, why are you in a bathroom? Why can't you talk in the office?'

Raphael shifted in his chair. 'Things are rather delicate at the moment. I don't want people to know anything unusual is going on, in London or anywhere else. It may jeopardise the work I'm doing.'

'What work are you doing?'

That closed expression again. 'I can't discuss that right now. All in good time, Jemma.' Then he sighed. 'Should I come back?'

Jemma considered the question. *I wish you would*, she thought. *I wish you'd come back, take this mess out of my hands, get rid of Lennox and tell me what to do.* But that wasn't the question he had asked. 'I can manage,' she said. 'I may need to talk to you more often, though. Things are getting strange.'

'Things are generally pretty strange,' said Raphael. 'But yes, the current situation is unusual, even in my experience.'

Oddly, Jemma found that reassuring. *At least I'm not over-dramatising things. As long as it isn't really the end of the world.* 'So I should continue searching for Drusilla, and keep watching out at the British Library,' she said.

'That's right,' said Raphael. 'And name the kittens.' He held up his hands as she glared at him. 'It was a joke.'

A customer opened the door and looked round it at Jemma.

'Yes, do come in,' she said. 'I'd better go, I have a customer.'

'I had better go, too,' said Raphael, 'or people will wonder what on earth I had for lunch. Bye, Jemma.' The screen turned black.

'Do you need any help?' Jemma asked the customer, an elderly man wearing a tweed jacket and a matching hat with fishing flies stuck in the band. She closed the laptop and put it away.

'Would you happen to have a copy of Montaigne's *Complete Essays?*' he asked.

'Let me check.' Jemma consulted the shop database. 'We did, but unfortunately we sold it last week. I could look out for a copy next time I replenish the stock, but if you don't want to wait you could try Burns Books down the road. They have a large non-fiction selection, bigger than here.' When she had taken over the shop it had been entirely non-fiction, since Brian, its previous owner, disapproved of fiction. Jemma had made it her business to make the bookshop a very different place.

'Jolly good, I'll go there. Thank you.' He tipped his hat to her and went on his way.

Jemma left the counter and roamed around the shop, neatening the shelves and moving a few books that had been put in the wrong place. Maddy usually kept on top of that, which meant it must have been a busy morning. *Hopefully with good sales*, she thought, and opened the till. That didn't tell her much, so she checked card transactions. Those looked much healthier, and she smiled. *You don't need some half-baked philosophy to sell books. I'll do my best to make sure that Luke and Em aren't forced to waste their time on fool's errands.* She glanced at her watch. Lennox and Ben were probably moving on to their main course at the nice little Italian place. No doubt there would be a glass of wine, or possibly two, and a pudding, and coffee. She caught sight of her expression in the computer screen: she appeared positively malevolent. *There isn't much you can do about them*, she told herself. *Keep your own house in order, Jemma. That's what's important.*

Then she remembered Raphael's question: how the knowledge emergencies they had dealt with connected to recent events. She fetched the *London A-Z*, found maps of the City of London wards on the internet, and started a list of notable buildings or monuments which stood on or near a boundary. She reached the bottom of the page before she had gone through more than five wards. *This is ridiculous*, she thought, laying down her pen, which was immediately seized by the ginger kitten for a game of bat-the-random-object. 'You can probably make better use of that than me,' she told him. Instead she made a cup of tea and ate her salad and hummus sandwich, though she barely tasted it. *It's impossible to keep track of all these places. The next event could happen anywhere. It's like playing whack-a-

mole with hundreds of holes to watch and a broken mallet. The odds are definitely not in my favour.

Maddy came in, looking frazzled. She took off her coat and bag and hung them up without speaking.

'Have you had a break?' asked Jemma.

'It hasn't stopped,' said Maddy. 'Ben rang the shop and said he wanted us to change the window display. Something about books with April in the title. Then he rang again twenty minutes later and said he'd had a better idea and we had to fill the window with blue books.'

'Blue books? Did he say why?'

'He began explaining, but I'm afraid I couldn't bear to listen, so I rustled a paper bag near the receiver and told him the line was bad, then hung up.' She bit her lip.

Jemma laughed. 'If I'd thought of it, I would have done exactly the same.' She got up. 'I'll put the kettle on. How are Luke and Em?'

'Mutinous,' Maddy replied. 'Em says that the coffee machine is refusing to make espressos.'

Jemma made a face. 'Can't think why.'

The shop phone rang and they both looked at it warily. 'I'll get it,' said Jemma. 'If I raise a finger, pass me a paper bag.'

Maddy giggled. 'Message received and understood.'

Jemma braced herself and answered the phone. 'Good afternoon, the Friendly Bookshop.'

'Ah, so you're in,' said Sergeant Hawkins. 'I was in two minds whether to phone the shop or try your mobile, since you're out and about so much that I doubt you spend any time at work.'

Jemma leaned on the counter. 'Does that mean you're pulling me in for an interview?'

'I wish I had the time,' the sergeant replied, in a bitter tone. 'As you enjoy hanging around in London, I thought you might be interested to learn that the River Walbrook has burst its banks. It's a stone's throw from where you were this morning.'

'The River Walbrook?' asked Jemma. *Isn't the Thames the only river in London?*

'Yes, the River Walbrook,' Sergeant Hawkins replied. 'I'm surprised you don't know it, as you seem to know so much about everything else. That being the case, I'd appreciate it if you'd meet me there ASAP. And that isn't a request. It's an order.'

Chapter 9

As the train eased its way into Mansion House station, Jemma had a distinct feeling of déjà vu. She disembarked, wondering how she would know where to find the river.

She needn't have worried, as an announcement came over the tannoy. 'We regret to inform you that there is a flooding incident in the Walbrook area. Please keep to the marked routes and do not go behind the barriers. Thank you.'

She emerged into daylight and was confronted with a sign which said *ROAD CLOSED – PLEASE TAKE CARE*, with an arrow pointing to the left. So she followed it.

She found Sergeant Hawkins directing operations, now in uniform, with a peaked cap, and equipped with a high-vis jacket and a megaphone. 'Please respect the barriers,' he shouted at two people who were hanging over them, filming both him and the rushing water. Jemma waved and he scowled at her, then beckoned her with his free hand.

'Good afternoon,' she said, coming to a stop at the barrier. 'This isn't the flood I was expecting.' She gestured at the water, which could best have been described as a fast-flowing stream.

'We've got pumps working on it,' Sergeant Hawkins said, through the megaphone. She winced and he lowered it. 'Sorry.'

'Why have you dragged me across London again?' she said. 'What am I supposed to know?'

'If I knew that, I wouldn't bother asking you, would I?' said Sergeant Hawkins. 'I'm working on the basis that anyone who happens to be in the right place to receive a mysterious tip-off about a crime is probably implicated.'

'I didn't even know there was a River Walbrook,' said Jemma.

'It's usually underground,' Sergeant Hawkins replied. 'They boxed it in at some point because it was getting in the way. Like an old pipe spoiling your nice new bathroom.' He said it without emotion. 'So what were you doing round here this morning? I've checked, and as far as I can tell there's no reason for a bookshop manager to be in the vicinity of St Stephen Walbrook.'

Jemma gazed at the water flowing no more than a foot from her baseball boots. 'Why have you put these barriers up?' she asked. 'It seems pretty minor.'

'Public health,' said the police officer. 'It's come from underground, and there's all sorts down there you probably wouldn't want to think about. Sewers aren't the half of it.'

Jemma remembered the occasion when Em's ex-boyfriend, Damon, had almost been drowned in an underground river, emerging soaked and terrified. 'Fair point,' she said.

'It is,' said Sergeant Hawkins. 'And you're changing the subject. What *were* you doing here this morning? I'd appreciate a straight answer, if you don't mind. I already know you have a knack for being in the wrong place at the right time, so to speak.'

It was on the tip of her tongue to tell him. It would be such a relief to tell the truth, to share the burden with someone who might be able to help and was right there, not out to lunch or doing something top secret in Italy. But the need for secrecy about the Keepers' Guild filled her mind.

'How do I know you're a bona-fide police officer?' she asked. 'Half the time you're not in uniform, and to be honest, that doesn't look like a proper police uniform. The colours are wrong.'

'That's because you're used to Met Police uniforms,' Sergeant Hawkins said flatly. 'This is a City of London police uniform. It's different.'

'What's your police number, then? What division are you? Have you got some form of ID on you?' He glared at her. 'I'm pretty sure you have to produce your ID if someone asks you.'

'I don't believe this,' he muttered, fishing in his pockets. Eventually he drew out a small black card holder and flipped it open. 'Satisfied?'

Jemma studied the card, which confirmed that Michael Hawkins was a sergeant in the City of London Police, Extramural Activities Division. She took a mental note of his number, just in case, then nodded, and he put it away. 'What's the extramural activities division?' she asked.

'What do you do?'

'Anything outside the remit of the other divisions,' he replied. 'We're the any other duties squad.' From the speed of his answer, she suspected both that he'd used it before, and that it wasn't true.

'Such as?'

He waved a hand at the water. 'Underground rivers escaping. Rock theft. Loiterers in libraries.'

'None of those things are connected,' said Jemma.

'Aren't they?' he asked, and she felt her face warm up. She hoped it wasn't having a visible effect.

'Ahoy there!' A tall, thin man with a long grey beard, wearing an Indiana Jones hat and a survival vest with multiple pockets, strode towards them. 'Looks like you have it under control...' He peered at the police officer's shoulder, 'Sergeant Hawkins, I presume. I'm not entirely sure you need me.'

The two people Sergeant Hawkins had rebuked earlier began filming the new arrival. He took off his hat and bowed to them, then addressed Sergeant Hawkins. 'When did this begin?'

'One of the office buildings reported a leak an hour ago,' said the sergeant. 'They phoned the water company thinking it was a burst pipe, but when an engineer arrived he realised what it was and got in touch.' Jemma wondered how the engineer had known who to contact. 'What started it, Percy?'

'Hang on,' said Jemma, 'haven't I seen you on TV?'

'You might have,' he said, scratching the side of his nose. 'Percy Caldwell, geologist, dowser, and underground river expert.' He extended a long brown hand, which she shook. It was surprisingly warm; she had expected it to be cold and clammy, by association.

'The flood,' said Sergeant Hawkins. 'What caused it?'

'Rivers rise for a reason,' said Percy Caldwell. 'The usual reason is heavy rainfall which the river bed cannot contain. However, given that the last few weeks have been dry, we can rule that out. Another possibility is a blockage in one of the Walbrook's many tributaries, which could cause a diversion in the river and force it above ground.' He bent to peer at the clear water. 'I'm aware you have pumps further up, Sergeant, but I would have expected more force to the flow. I shall have to investigate further before I can give you a definite answer.'

Upstream, to their left, screams and exclamations burst forth. 'Excuse me a moment,' said Percy, and loped towards the source of the noise. When he returned a few minutes later he was holding a human skull, dripping with water. It looked ancient: most of the teeth were missing and there was a hole in the top, by which he was carrying it. 'Don't worry, it isn't new. The Walbrook has a habit of throwing up skulls every so often. It's been doing it for hundreds of years, and it's typical of a river such as this to spit one out now.' He turned the skull to face him and smiled fondly at it. 'There are all sorts of legends about the Walbrook skulls, but sadly for folklorists, this one has probably escaped from a cemetery.'

'Are there legends about the river?' asked Jemma. She half-expected Sergeant Hawkins to tell her to be quiet and stop asking irrelevant questions, but when she glanced at him he was gazing at Percy, his hand on the pocket where she suspected he kept his notebook.

Percy blew air through his pursed lips. 'Where do you want me to start? The river is as old as time, more or less, and before they forced it underground it was one of the most important rivers in London. It split the city in two, a hill on each side, and it divided the city in more ways than the merely geographical. On that side' – he waved an arm – 'rich people and land-based trade. On the other side, poor people struggling to make a living from the river.' He gazed into the distance with a faraway expression. 'Perhaps they thought that forcing the river into culverts and building over it would remove the division; but every so often the river bubbles up again. You can only bottle something up for so long; eventually, it breaks free.'

'Wow,' said one of the people filming Percy, lowering his phone. 'That's, like, wisdom for life.'

Jemma's head swam, and she put her hand on the barrier. Suddenly it was difficult to breathe. *That's ridiculous. I'm outside. There's plenty of air.*

'Are you all right?' said Sergeant Hawkins, looking at her suspiciously. 'You've gone a funny colour.'

'It's the skull,' Jemma gasped out. 'I'm squeamish about things like that.'

His mouth twisted. 'But flying books and weird smoke and paranormal activity is fine.'

'I wouldn't say that,' she replied. The words were difficult to form; her mouth felt numb.

He put a hand in his pocket. Jemma was expecting him to bring out his notebook, but instead he handed her a boiled sweet in crackly cellophane wrapping. 'Suck on that,' he said. 'I'll be back in a couple of minutes.' He headed to a café and returned with a cup which she knew would contain disgustingly sweet tea.

She took it and gazed at him. 'Do I have to?' She had to talk around the boiled sweet lodged in her cheek, but the numbness was dissipating.

'Yes, you do,' said Sergeant Hawkins. 'The last thing I need is for someone to fall, hit their head and sue me.' But his tone was considerably less brusque than his words.

She sipped the tea. 'I'll sit over there,' she said, 'if you don't mind.' He followed her gaze to a set of white stone steps. Most were occupied with sightseers busy on their phones, but there was room for her.

'Off you go then,' he said. 'Do you need a hand?'

Jemma shook her head. 'I'll be fine.' She looked up at him. 'Thanks for the tea.' She made her way slowly to the steps and sat down, feeling the cold stone through her jeans. She took the lid off the tea and sipped carefully. *Thank heavens for that skull.* Without it, there would have been no way to explain her reaction. A river that marked a division, a boundary – and now it had forced its way above ground. *Don't step on the cracks*, she thought, and shivered. *I don't know what's going on, and I'm not sure I want to. But one thing's for certain. This – all this – is about more than books. And I have no idea how to fix it.*

She saw Sergeant Hawkins's beady brown eyes studying her, and hastily bent her head to her drink.

Chapter 10

Jemma got slowly to her feet, still clutching her cup of tea, and took a few experimental steps. Her knees held, and her head remained clear.

She glanced at the scene beyond the barriers. People were drifting away, since there was nothing new to see and the pumps were doing their job. Sergeant Hawkins was standing, hands in pockets, watching Percy Caldwell, who was staring at the dial of a complicated-looking instrument. She considered sneaking off, but decided with regret that she ought to at least thank the sergeant for the tea. *I hope he won't insist on me giving a statement now.*

He watched her move carefully towards him. 'Feeling better?'

'A bit,' said Jemma. 'I'd better get back to the shop. I left in rather a rush.'

'Yeah, sorry about that.' He did actually appear shamefaced. 'I probably shouldn't have summoned you, but it seemed too much of a coincidence.'

Jemma shrugged. 'In your position, I'd probably have

done the same thing.' She managed to pull the corners of her mouth up, though it felt more like an effort than a smile. 'Anyway, I'll be off.' She considered saying goodbye to Percy, but he was intent on his gadget. 'Will you let me know if you discover anything?'

Sergeant Hawkins gave her a beady glare. 'I might do. It depends.'

'On what?'

'On whether I think you should know or not.'

Jemma raised an eyebrow. 'Why? Do I look dangerous?'

He snorted. 'If I did my job based purely on who looked dangerous I wouldn't be much of a police officer, would I? Off you go.'

Feeling summarily dismissed, Jemma trudged back the way she had come, to Mansion House station. But when she reached it her feet slowed, and she practically had to will herself to the ticket barrier. She took out her purse. *There are skulls down there*, she thought.

The train travels through a sealed tube, she told herself. *You're being ridiculous.* She pulled out her card.

Boundaries are changing. Rivers are rising. It isn't safe.

'Excuse me,' said a voice behind her, which belonged to a person clearly in a hurry. 'Are you going through this barrier, or what?'

Jemma scurried away. 'Make your blooming mind up!' someone called after her, and laughed.

Jemma emerged into the open air wondering what to do next. She could walk, but that would take too long. *Would a bus take me part of the way?* She went to the nearest bus stop and consulted the timetable, but couldn't make head or tail of it. In the end, she walked in what she hoped was the right direction until she saw a taxi with its light on and flagged it down.

She stared out of the window to make sure the driver didn't talk to her, and tried to think. Why had the River Walbrook chosen to break out now? Yes, it was near the London Stone, or where the stone was supposed to be, but while the Mithraeum and the Samaritans' phone had both given a warning, the river couldn't do that. 'Unless you count the skull,' she said. The taxi driver eyed her in the rear-view mirror, and she realised she had spoken aloud.

When the taxi reached the Friendly Bookshop she got a receipt, then took a deep breath before letting herself out of the cab and walking into the shop. Maddy was serving a customer who had put a matched set of *The Lord of the Rings* on the counter. She touched the books every few seconds, as if to make sure they were still there. 'I've been searching for this edition for months,' she said, running her hand over the topmost book.

Jemma smiled. How lovely to have no problem more pressing than finding a particular edition of a book. *You don't know that*, she told herself. *She could have all sorts of things going on in her life.*

'All OK?' she said to Maddy, taking off her jacket and hanging it up.

'Yes, fine,' said Maddy, going through the books and slipping them into a paper bag. She smiled at the customer. 'Is it because of the sprayed edges?' she asked.

'It has special endpapers, too,' said the customer,

proudly. 'But yes, the sprayed edges were a factor. It's a present for a friend.'

'A good friend, I take it,' said Maddy.

'Yes. She is,' said the woman. She bit her lip, and her cheeks were slightly pinker than before.

Jemma watched Maddy deal with the customer, and wondered vaguely whether she should have bothered coming back. *Maddy can manage without me.* 'Shall I put the kettle on?' she asked.

'Please,' said Maddy.

Jemma went through to the back room and flicked the kettle on. *I could stay here and do research, or even go upstairs. Maddy could text me if it gets really busy.* While that was true, though, she knew she would be too guilty to concentrate, always looking at her phone and listening for noise in the shop downstairs.

Luna sashayed into the kitchen, paused to accept fuss from Jemma, then went to her bowl and ate some biscuits. 'Don't tell me you've finished the food upstairs,' said Jemma.

Luna gazed at her with huge green eyes and uttered a short, squeaky meow.

'Have you come downstairs for peace and quiet?' Luna bent her head to her bowl and purred gently as she crunched biscuits, which Jemma took as a yes. *Imagine having four kittens to bring up.* No wonder Luna seemed to spend more time in her basket these days.

The noise from the kettle grew and Jemma remembered her duty. She made the tea, gave Luna one more fuss for luck, and took the mugs through. Maddy's customer had departed, and she was sitting on the high stool behind the counter, looking earnestly at Jemma. 'How did it go? What did the police officer want?'

'He admitted he probably shouldn't have dragged me over there,' said Jemma, putting Maddy's mug on the counter.

'So why did he? What happened? You seem exhausted.'

'Thanks.' Jemma sipped her tea. 'Nothing much. Percy Caldwell was there, investigating why the river had flooded. You know, the bearded guy off the telly.'

'Oooh!' squealed Maddy. 'Did you get his autograph?'

'No, I didn't. Sorry. I'm quite tired.'

'Is that why you came back in a taxi?'

Inwardly, Jemma cursed Maddy's sharp eyes. 'Mostly, plus it saved time.'

'Did you find anything out?'

'There wasn't much to see,' Jemma replied. 'It wasn't a big flood. But there was something weird. Percy Caldwell said the River Walbrook used to separate the two halves of the city, as a natural boundary, before it was forced underground.'

'A boundary?' said Maddy. 'Like the ones between the wards of the city? Luke mentioned you'd asked,' she said, in response to Jemma's raised eyebrows.

'That's what I was thinking,' said Jemma. 'I'm glad it isn't just me.'

'What are you going to do?'

'I don't know. Research, I suppose.'

'One thing sticks out a mile,' said Maddy.

'Does it?' Jemma looked at her, eyebrows raised.

'You'll have to enlighten me.'

'Well, you've just visited a river in flood, and River Logistics?'

Jemma slapped her forehead. 'Of course! I mean, they might not even be connected, but—'

'But it's worth a look?'

'Absolutely. Thanks, Maddy.'

'No problem.'

Jemma fetched her laptop and headed into the back room. 'Call me if you need me.'

Forty minutes later, she was not much wiser about River Logistics. She had visited the website, of course, as she had done several times before, and pored over the information – the board of directors, the areas the company specialised in, and all the documentation she could find, which wasn't much.

The company had been founded by two brothers, John and Joseph Shore, in 1972. Their faces beamed from the Executive Team webpage: one thin, one portly, but both white-haired and dressed in slightly incongruous matching grey suits. They still ran the company jointly, and it operated throughout the Greater London area. Jemma wondered whether it was worth checking Companies House for more information, then remembered Em had already done that and found nothing of interest. 'Of course she didn't,' she said aloud. 'If you were up to no good, you'd hardly advertise it.'

Presumably they did advertise it somewhere, though – otherwise how would Drusilla have known to use the company? Unless they were entirely innocent pawns in her game. But the link to the River Walbrook made her doubt that.

Drusilla... Where is she? And how did she get her powers back – or some powers, anyway? Jemma cast the second question aside as too difficult, and returned to the first. *Is she still in London? Or could she have returned to Berkshire, and be in hiding there?* She knew from their research that Drusilla's house had been sold, but that gave no clue as to where she was now. Could she have visited her old bookshop? There might be resources there that would help her. A useful book, or something about the shop itself. *Don't say I've let her slip through my fingers and grow stronger while I've been chasing everything else...*

Jemma opened a new tab in her browser and typed furiously, and a minute later she was dialling a number on her phone.

'Good afternoon, Chapters Bookshop,' said an urbane male voice.

'Is that Marcus?' she asked.

'It is! And you are?'

'Jemma James. You probably don't remember me, but —'

'Of course I do! You interviewed me for the post at Burns Books.'

'That's right, yes. You have an excellent memory.' She half-expected him to say *Yes, I do*, but instead he laughed.

'It wasn't so very long ago. What can I do for you, Jemma?'

'This is probably an odd question, but you haven't seen

a woman called Drusilla Davenport in the shop lately, have you?'

'I haven't come across anyone of that name, no.'

'She's well dressed with highlighted blonde hair, posh and haughty looking, in what appears to be late middle age. Oh, and she might have one wrist bandaged.'

'Doesn't ring a bell,' said Marcus.

'Has anyone come in with a bandaged wrist?'

'Er... I don't remember anyone,' said Marcus. 'May I ask what this concerns?'

'I know it sounds ridiculous,' said Jemma, 'but Raphael and I are trying to track her down. She used to own your bookshop, so I wondered if you'd seen her.'

'I can ask my staff,' said Marcus. 'If one of us does bump into her, would you like us to pass on a message?'

'Oh gosh, no,' said Jemma. 'Don't do that, and don't mention me or Raphael. Just tell me that you've seen her.'

'Right,' said Marcus. She could almost hear him frowning. 'It's been lovely to speak to you, Jemma, but the shop is quite busy—'

'I'm sure it is. Thanks, Marcus. Bye.' Jemma ended the call and stared at her phone. *He probably thinks I've gone doolally. And if I was on his end of the phone call, I'd probably think the same.*

Chapter 11

That evening, Jemma watched the ginger kitten chase its tail, running in circles, and wondered if she was doing exactly the same in a metaphorical sense. *What if Drusilla has stopped her activities, and I'm pushing everyone to do pointless things?* Then she remembered the London Stone and the overflowing River Walbrook. *Who's behind that, if not Drusilla?*

She had planned to cook a proper meal for a change, but after flicking through several cookbooks and examining the contents of her cupboards and fridge, she could settle on nothing that appealed. *You could make that risotto*, she thought, then caught sight of the still-circling kitten, imagined herself endlessly stirring, and went to Nafisa's mini-market, where she bought a microwave curry and a can of Diet Coke.

'Haven't seen you for a few days,' said Nafisa, as she scanned Jemma's shopping. 'What happened to the healthy eating? This is not a proper meal.' She tapped the packet. 'Look at all that saturated fat. And salt.'

'Why do you sell it, then?'

Nafisa shrugged. 'Customers buy it. I tell them they shouldn't, but they ignore me. Card or phone?'

Jemma held her phone to the reader and escaped with her purchases, unsure whether to feel more guilty for not cooking, eating rubbish, or knowing that with her Keeper powers, she could eat what she liked with impunity.

That night she slept badly, despite or perhaps because of the array of cats on her bed. On one hand they were soft and comforting; on the other they arranged themselves in a way which made it impossible to change position without upsetting a furry body, which would tumble into another and provoke an outraged squeak at the very least. She settled herself down, apologising to the cats involved in the incident, but still thoughts raced around her head. Nothing useful, of course – just vague ideas which she knew she would have forgotten by the morning. Or if she did remember them, they would seem ridiculous in the cold light of day. Occasionally she dozed, then awoke with a start, dreaming that she had fallen off a precipice while being chased by Sergeant Hawkins, or worse, had stepped on a crack in the pavement and plummeted into the depths of London where the skulls lived.

At last it was morning. Jemma made herself an extremely strong cup of coffee, fed the cats, and got herself more or less ready to face the day. But it wasn't just the day that she had to face. She had contemplated phoning Raphael again, but she didn't want to bother him until she had something more concrete than suspicions. *I need help*, she thought, staring at the bags under her eyes in the mirror. *I can't do this alone.*

She went downstairs at eight thirty to get the shop ready to open, and Maddy arrived ten minutes later. 'Rough night?' she asked, gazing at Jemma.

'Is it so obvious?' She had done her best to perk herself up, taking a long hot shower and putting on make-up to disguise her haggardness. Clearly, it hadn't worked.

'Sorry,' said Maddy. 'You need a day off.'

'Probably,' said Jemma. 'Unfortunately, it isn't that sort of job at the moment. But I made a decision this morning.'

Maddy gave her a wary look. 'What sort of decision?'

'I'm going to Burns Books and asking Lennox for help. Or Ben, if Lennox isn't there.'

'Help? Those two?'

'Not so much from them, more that they spend more time in the shop so that Luke and Em aren't so busy. Then they could help me work out what's going on. And they could help here, so that you're not always stuck minding the shop when I dash off.'

Maddy smiled. 'That would be good. It can't hurt to ask.'

'That's what I figured. Anyway, let's get ready to open. There's no point in going yet; I doubt either of them will be in before quarter past nine at the earliest.'

The hands of the grandfather clock ticked round slowly. Jemma had occupied herself with perhaps the only thing that could make the prospect of asking a favour from Lennox seem appealing: going through the shop's income and outgoings from the previous month. Eventually, though, that dismal task was complete, and she got up. 'It's now or never, I guess.'

'Good luck,' said Maddy. 'I hope you won't need it.'

'So do I.' Jemma raised a hand in farewell as she left the shop, wondering why she felt as if she were going on an expedition from which she might never return, rather than popping down the road to have a chat with her boss.

She could hear Lennox talking beneath the jangle of the bell as she pushed open the door of the bookshop. 'That will be the subject of my next monograph,' he concluded, leaning forward slightly. He turned to see who had entered. 'Ah, Jemma. Ben and I were just talking about you.' He waved a hand at Ben, who smirked.

'Were you?' She glanced at Luke, who was standing behind the shop counter. He wore the expression of someone who had chosen a chocolate truffle and found out too late that it was a coffee cream.

'Indeed we were,' said Lennox. 'I was saying to Ben that perhaps we ought to consider recruiting another member of staff.'

'Oh good,' said Jemma. 'That relates to what I want to ask you.'

'Does it?' Lennox immediately looked suspicious.

'Yes,' Jemma replied. 'So if you'd like me to help you recruit somebody, I would absolutely be up for that.'

'Mmm,' said Lennox. 'What were you planning to ask me, Jemma?'

Jemma debated which approach would work best, and opted for humility. 'As you know, I've been running the patrol at the British Library, and investigating the odd things that have happened in London.'

'Yeees?' His eyes narrowed.

'But, to be honest, combining that with running the Friendly Bookshop is tiring me out, even with Maddy's invaluable help. There isn't time in the day to chase every lead, try to anticipate Drusilla's next move, and do a good job of running the bookshop. So I wondered if Luke and perhaps Em would be able to help.'

'That's fine with me,' said Luke. 'I'm sure Em will say the same.'

'You shouldn't speak for your colleague,' said Lennox. 'And while it may be fine with you – both of you – I'm not so sure it's fine with me.'

'But if you're thinking of recruiting a new staff member —'

'I meant someone more senior,' said Lennox. 'They could oversee the day-to-day running of the bookshop while Ben and I are out on business.'

Jemma stared at him. 'That's part of Ben's job.'

'It has been bundled with the Assistant Keeper role, certainly,' said Lennox. 'However, Ben's role could be executed more fully if we had someone to carry the administrative load, so to speak.'

'What about London?' cried Jemma. 'Weird stuff is happening every day. I can't keep up with it on my own!'

'Did anyone ask you to?' said Lennox. 'I mean, I'm sure it's fascinating to dash around investigating strange happenings, but does it have any bearing on finding Drusilla? Are we sure she even presents a problem any more?'

'An underground river flooded today!' Jemma gave him

her hardest stare. 'And for all I know, something else will happen tomorrow, and the day after, and the day after that.'

'Then maybe you should let it happen,' said Lennox. 'It isn't any of your business, Jemma.'

'It is my business!' Jemma heard her voice rising. 'It has to be,' she said, more quietly. 'A police officer is looking into it too, but he doesn't know what's going on either.'

'There!' Lennox exclaimed triumphantly. 'The police are aware of it, so you don't need to get involved. Splendid.' He winked at Ben. 'So if you could dig out the manager's job description, Jemma, Ben and I can move forward.'

Jemma ran her hands through her hair. Behind the counter, Luke's thumbs were flying over his phone screen. 'What do I have to say to make you understand, Lennox?'

'Dr Nash, please,' said Lennox.

'Oh, for heaven's sake! This is more important than your stupid title. If something happens to the city because you wouldn't spare the resources to save it, how will you be able to swan around London acting as if you own the place? Tell me that.'

Lennox bristled. 'You should apologise, Jemma, for speaking to me in such a rude manner.'

'Frankly, you deserve it. You're supposed to be the acting Keeper of England, the Guild's head representative in this country. You're abusing your position and shirking your duties. You ought to be ashamed of yourself.'

Em appeared in the opening which led to the back room. 'I, um, heard a noise and wondered what was going on.' *So that's who Luke was texting.*

'Jemma's asked if we can help with her investigation,' said Luke.

'Yes, of course,' said Em.

'Absolutely not,' said Lennox. 'I would have said no anyway, but after that outburst—'

'Who's with me?' Jemma said quietly. She looked from Luke to Em, and back again.

'I am,' said Luke.

'Me too,' said Em.

'I'm warning you both,' said Lennox. 'Your duty is to me, and to the shop. If you disobey me, I shall have to think carefully about whether you still have jobs. Plenty of people would be glad to work here.'

Luke came out from behind the counter and fetched his coat. 'Oh, wait a minute,' he said, looking slightly worried.

'Second thoughts, eh?' said Lennox, smiling.

Luke went into the back room and returned with a Tupperware box. 'I didn't want to leave my lunch behind. Trust me, you wouldn't like it.'

Em unhooked her denim jacket and slipped it on. 'This doesn't have to be a fight, Lennox.'

'*Dr Nash!*' thundered Lennox, his face red.

'Whatever.' Em picked up her bag. 'Ready when you are, Jemma.'

'Marvellous.' Jemma grinned. 'Good luck with your recruitment, Dr Nash.' And she walked out of the shop with Luke and Em feeling that it might not be such a bad day after all.

Chapter 12

Maddy was alone when Jemma entered the Friendly Bookshop. 'How did it go— Oh!' she exclaimed as Luke and Em followed Jemma in. 'It went well, then.'

'That depends on your point of view,' said Jemma.

'We walked out,' said Luke. He said it matter-of-factly, as if it had been the obvious thing to do.

'You walked out?' said Maddy. 'What did Lennox say?'

'He didn't give us much choice,' said Em.

Jemma spread her hands. 'When I turned up, he said he was thinking of recruiting someone. What he meant was a manager, so that he and Ben can have more spare time. Luke and Em would have been even more tied to the bookshop, because you can bet any manager they recruit would go off with them instead of doing any work.'

'I see,' said Maddy. 'I mean, I'm pleased you're here, but… Anyway, I'll get the kettle on.' She went through to the back room, and Jemma was sure that she heard a faint sigh.

'What's the plan?' said Luke. 'Where do we start?'

'That's a good question,' said Jemma. 'To be honest, I'm not sure. I've been struggling to do what I can for so long that I haven't considered what we could do with more time or resources. I'll tell you what happened yesterday, to bring you up to speed.' Quickly, she summarised the previous day's events: the phone call in St Stephen Walbrook that had diverted her from the Mithraeum, the theft of the fake London Stone, the overflowing underground river, her realisation about the boundaries, and her fruitless phone call to Marcus.

'That's as far as I could get on my own,' she said, as Maddy came in with a tea tray. 'But now you're here. The only thing is…'

'What?' asked Em.

'Well, most of the books we've been using for research are in the stockroom at Burns Books. I'm not sure how we can get hold of those; we're probably not welcome.'

'Ah,' said Luke, frowning. 'That might be a problem.'

'It'll be OK,' said Em. 'We've made a stand today, but Luke and I haven't actually resigned or been fired. We've come to help you out.'

'I'm not entirely sure Lennox will see it that way,' said Jemma. 'He looked pretty cross when we left.'

'You were quite rude to him,' said Em. 'Obviously he deserved it, but he won't see that.'

'You'll suggest we pour oil on troubled waters, I suppose,' said Jemma. She felt her lip curl, and forced it back down. 'I have no intention of apologising.'

'You won't have to,' said Em. 'Not yet, anyway. The thing is, right now those two are in the bookshop on their own. I imagine after an hour or so they'll be delighted if one of us returns, says we will come back but not yet, and happens to borrow some books from the stockroom. We could even ask for the books and let them think they've bargained us into coming back.'

'That's sneaky,' said Jemma. 'I like it.' She sighed. 'I guess this is why I was never really management material. Not sneaky enough.'

Em grinned. 'You don't have to be sneaky to be a manager,' she said. 'Though sometimes it helps. Let's get on with what we can, and one of us can pop over later.'

'I hate to interrupt your plans for world domination,' said Maddy, putting the tray on the counter, 'but in the rare event that we do have a customer this morning, who's looking after the shop? Where's this investigation going to happen? You can't use the counter.'

'We'll use the back room,' said Jemma. 'That way we can all talk to each other and swap places when it's someone else's turn to mind the shop. And if we stay here, the other bookshop will know we're working on the problem.' She felt a pang for Burns Books, left alone with Lennox and Ben in charge. 'I hope those two don't reorganise everything and make a mess.'

'They won't,' said Maddy, and her lip curled enough for two. 'That would involve lifting a finger. They're probably eating their way through the cake display as we speak.'

'They aren't,' said Em. She felt in her pocket and held up a key. 'I locked the cupboards before I left and switched everything off. If they want anything from the café, they'll have to be nice. Oh yes, and I brought supplies.' She reached into her tote and retrieved a brown-paper bag.

'Cinnamon rolls? Em, you're the best.' Luke took the bag from her, opened it and extracted a roll. 'I'll do the first shift on the till. You've been chained to it for days, Maddy, it's only fair.'

'Thank you,' said Maddy, and stood on tiptoe to kiss him on the cheek.

The cat flap banged open and four kittens raced in, practically nose to tail. They chased each other in circles, then suddenly stopped and stared at everyone. Luna strolled in, followed by Folio, who issued a short, sharp meow, and the kittens scampered to his side.

'I would never have thought of Folio as a disciplinarian,' said Em.

'I guess parenthood does funny things to people – I mean cats,' Jemma replied. She turned to the kittens, who regarded her with saucer-like eyes. 'I don't mind you being here, but you must be quiet and not trip people up. Is that clear?'

The ginger kitten made a dash under one of the shelves, but the tortoiseshell kitten chased him out and shepherded him back to Folio. 'Thank you,' said Jemma, and the tortoiseshell kitten squeaked.

The shop door opened and Felicity peeped round it. 'Oh, are you having a meeting?'

'We're just finishing,' said Jemma. 'How can we help?' Then she thought for a moment. 'Don't you usually go to Burns Books?'

'I do,' said Felicity. 'I was there a moment ago, but as soon as I opened the door Dr Nash came striding over and said they weren't open due to staffing difficulties.' She eyed Luke and Em.

'I'm not sure why they said that,' said Jemma. 'After all, there are two of them. But yes, we are definitely open. Luke can help you if you've got a specific enquiry, or go ahead and browse.'

'It's a birthday present for Jerome, actually,' said Felicity. 'I don't suppose you can remember which Asimov books he has? I meant to take a photo last time I was round at his flat, but I forgot.'

'I'll look on the database,' said Luke.

Felicity exhaled and leaned against the counter. 'Thank you so much. I shouldn't have left it till the last minute, but you know how it is.'

'We'll let you get on,' said Jemma, and picking up the tray, she led the others to the back room.

Three quarters of an hour later, they had a big map of London Blu-Tacked to the wall, with stickers and Post-it notes marking significant locations, and Em was typing furiously on Jemma's laptop. 'You're right, Jemma,' she said, sitting back. 'There are so many important buildings situated on a ward boundary in the City of London that we couldn't monitor them all if we tried.'

'Did you get anywhere with River Logistics yesterday, Jemma?' asked Maddy.

'Nope,' said Jemma, 'but there's only really their website to go on, and Em has already checked Companies House. They seem to keep out of the news.'

'Which is suspicious in itself,' said Em. 'Look at DZD Holdings.'

'I'd almost forgotten about them,' said Jemma. 'Maybe we should see if anything new has been posted there.'

'Maybe we should,' said Em. 'There's something else to do first.' She smiled a slow smile. 'I reckon now is a good time to visit Burns Books and collect research materials.'

'Oh yes,' said Jemma. She grinned. 'That's assuming they haven't closed the shop and gone for an early lunch.'

'If I know Lennox,' said Em, 'he'll have a meeting in the diary which he simply has to attend. And he won't let Ben leave the shop in case we try to get in.' She rubbed her hands. 'The time is ripe. Do you want me to find anything in particular?'

'Just go into the stockroom and pick up the first box,' said Jemma. 'That will have everything we need.'

Em rolled her eyes. 'Of course.' She rose from her seat. 'If I'm not back in twenty minutes, maybe one of you should come and fetch me. I don't think Ben will take me hostage, but hey.'

'Make him an espresso and he'll be putty in your hands,' said Maddy.

'I may do that,' said Em, and with a wink, she left.

Maddy moved into her place by the laptop and began typing. 'What are you looking for?' asked Jemma.

'I was thinking about Percy Caldwell,' said Maddy.

'As you do.'

'No, I really like his stuff. He's got a YouTube channel with cool videos on folklore and superstitions.' She clicked the mousepad and Percy Caldwell's voice came out of the speaker. 'I'll put subtitles on,' she said, and muted the sound, then carried on typing. Occasionally she clicked the mousepad and engaged in more, shorter bursts of typing. Two minutes later: 'I knew it.' She stared at the screen with triumph in her eyes.

'You knew what?'

Maddy turned the laptop to face her. 'The head office of River Logistics is at 119a, Shoreditch High Street.' Percy Caldwell was strolling down a city street, mouthing silently. 'The video I put on is a walk he did along the River Walbrook. He starts from one of the sources of the river, in Shoreditch.'

'OK...'

'The walk begins at St Leonard's Church. I found its address, and it's at 119 Shoreditch High Street. It couldn't be closer if it tried. So River Logistics is based, to the best of our knowledge, at one of the sources of the River Walbrook.'

Jemma's head swam, and she took another cinnamon roll out of the bag. 'I don't believe it.'

'I do,' said Maddy, grimly.

They were still processing their discovery, and trying to work out how a courier company could have made an underground river rise, when Em rejoined them. 'Here you go,' she said, putting a box of books on the table. Then she looked at their faces. 'Are you two all right?'

'Maddy just made a discovery,' said Jemma. 'But how are you? How's the shop?'

Em smiled. 'As I suspected, Ben was alone. He was rather cross with me at first, but I apologised and said I was sure that things would blow over, and that seemed to cheer him up.' She flicked her hair and her smile broadened.

Jemma's eyes narrowed. 'Did you cast glamour on him?'

'Might have.' Then Em sighed. 'I need to get better at directing it. I was on my way out of the shop and some random man gave me a bunch of flowers. I tried to give them back, but he gave me a soppy look and hurried away. They're on the counter; I'll put them in water in a moment.'

'Did Ben say where Lennox had gone?' asked Jemma.

'To a meeting,' Maddy and Em chorused together, and burst out laughing.

'OK, I asked for that,' said Jemma, laughing too. Then her phone buzzed. 'Maybe that's him,' she said.

The display said *Hermione. Is it true you've resigned? I knew you were on a sabbatical, but I never thought you'd leave the bookshop.*

'What?!' Jemma shouted.

'What is it?' asked Maddy.

'Hermione just asked if I've resigned.'

Her phone buzzed again. *We don't speak much now you're not on committees*, Nina had texted, *but I didn't expect to hear you'd left through an official announcement.*

Jemma's grip tightened on the phone. 'Lennox has told the whole Guild that I've left.'

'But you haven't,' said Maddy. 'You're on secondment, everyone knows that.'

'Well, now they think I've gone.'

Another text, from Phil: *I've just seen the*

announcement, Jemma. Could you tell me who is now responsible for administering the library rota?

'I can't deal with this.' Jemma put the phone face down and ran her hands through her hair. She was tempted to clutch it, like a heroine in a melodrama. 'Lennox is probably sitting in his meeting and laughing his head off. Wait till I get my hands on him—'

The phone rang. It wasn't one of the special ringtones she had assigned to various people she knew, and when she turned the phone over, the display said *Number Withheld*. She was tempted to refuse the call, but fear of what might happen if she did made her press the *Answer* button.

'I never called you,' said a voice that sounded remarkably like Sergeant Hawkins. 'If I were you, I'd put a few essentials in a bag and get out sharpish.'

'Is that you, Sergeant Hawkins?'

'No, it isn't, and this isn't a phone call. Just do as I say if you value your freedom.'

Jemma put a hand to her head, which was beginning to throb. 'Why?'

'Because there's a pack of police officers on their way to arrest you. That's why.'

Chapter 13

'I don't understand,' Jemma said. She felt dizzy, as if she had been punched. 'Why are they coming to arrest me?'

'I'll give you the short version, since we're in a hurry,' said the person who claimed not to be Sergeant Hawkins. 'A woman came to the police station claiming that you assaulted her at the British Library. She showed the officer on duty a bruised wrist. The bruises were fading, but she had photos from the time of the incident. Very nasty indeed. At least one person is prepared to swear they saw you do it. Plus most of the library staff named you when your physical description was read out.'

'But I only grabbed her wrist,' said Jemma, 'and she was…'

You can't tell Guild secrets.

'She was what?'

'I can't tell you.'

'You won't tell me; that's an entirely different matter. And when the police cross-referenced this supposed attack with the description of the woman who shouldn't have been in that hoo-ha at the Maughan Library, they put two and two together. It's your call.' The phone went dead.

Jemma looked up and saw Em and Maddy staring at her, open-mouthed. 'What's going on?' asked Maddy, in a shocked whisper.

'Drusilla is getting me arrested for assaulting her,' said Jemma. 'The police are on their way. I need to do something.'

She ran upstairs to her flat. *Pack a few things*, he had said. She found a rucksack and stuffed in a couple of T-shirts and some underwear, toothbrush and toothpaste, a hairbrush, her notepad and two Pencils of Truth. *What else?* She glanced at her phone. *If I take that, they'll be able to track me. Lots of people have my number.*

She opened the drawer of her bedside table and took out the pay-as-you-go phone she had bought a few weeks before, when Lennox had blocked her mobile during work hours. It went into the rucksack. She glanced out of the window and saw, among the traffic crawling down Charing Cross Road, a police car. It was perhaps fifty metres away.

They're coming.

She remembered the hat and the glasses with plain lenses that she had worn when keeping a low profile after the Maughan Library incident. She found them and put them on, tucking her hair into the hat.

As she made for the door, the cats trooped through the cat flap and regarded her with grave eyes. 'Be good,' she whispered, stroking them each in turn. Then she ran downstairs. Someone must have told Luke in her absence, since he was goggling at her as if she had grown an extra head.

'I'm going,' she panted.

'Wait,' said Em. 'Where are you going?'

Jemma's shoulders drooped. 'I don't know, but I can't stay here. I can't fight Drusilla from inside a police cell, can I?' She eyed them, and suddenly stamped her foot. 'Help me! The police car's coming!'

'Then you can't go far,' said Luke. 'If they see someone run outside, or even hurry, they'll follow for sure. And you won't make it to a station. Not if they're within sight of the shop.'

Jemma put her purse into the rucksack and tried to think clearly, though panic gripped her brain with an iron hand. 'Em, come with me.'

'Of course, but where?'

'Burns Books; I need you to distract Ben.' She turned to the others. 'Mind the cats for me. And the books.'

Maddy nodded, swallowing, and Luke put an arm round her.

Jemma opened the shop door and peeped out. A lorry had stopped a few doors down and put its hazard lights on. The traffic behind it, presumably including the police car, was no longer visible. 'Let's go.' She hefted the rucksack and walked quickly towards Burns Books.

'What do you want me to do?' said Em, out of the side of her mouth.

'Keep Ben busy while I get to the stockroom.'

'OK, but...' Em gave her an odd, searching look. 'Will you hide in there?'

'Until I come up with something better,' said Jemma.

'Ben won't go in there, will he?'

'True,' said Em. She still seemed dubious. 'Maybe you can get into Raphael's flat, or sneak into the Tube when it's dark and they've gone.'

'Yes, that sounds good,' said Jemma, more to keep Em happy than because she thought it was a good plan. Then again, what was a good plan when you were running from the police? She couldn't even argue that she hadn't hurt Drusilla. *Technically, I'm guilty as sin. If I read about myself in the paper, I'd probably agree that I ought to be locked up.*

'Here we are,' said Em, as they reached the door of Burns Books. On it was pinned a notice written in angry capitals: *CLOSED DUE TO STAFF SHORTAGES. SORRY.* She pushed the door, which didn't move, and raised a hand to knock. 'Are you sure?'

'I'm sure,' said Jemma.

'Then here we go,' said Em, and rapped on the door. A teasing little smile played on her lips and her cheeks were faintly pink. *I have no idea how you do it*, thought Jemma, *but I'm glad you can.*

They heard footsteps, and Jemma moved out of sight of the door.

Ben opened it, looking extremely cross. 'Can't you read?' he snapped. Then he realised it was Em, and his expression softened immediately. 'Oh, it's you. I didn't think you were coming back.'

'Could I come in?' Em asked sweetly, toying with a strand of hair.

Ben staggered, then righted himself. 'Why yes, of

course. Sorry. I'm not cross with you, really I'm not. It's just a – difficult situation.'

'Oh yes, I agree,' said Em. 'I wondered whether we could discuss it. Perhaps over coffee downstairs?'

'That's a great idea!' exclaimed Ben.

'I'll come too,' said a man carrying a small dog, who had seen Em and stopped dead. 'I've no idea what you're talking about, but I'm willing to learn.'

Em stared at him, and the glamour she had been exerting on Ben was completely gone. The man took a step back, then shook his head and hurried away.

'Do come downstairs,' said Ben, leading the way. 'Oh, the door.'

'Don't worry, I'll get it,' said Em. 'I just need to, um, use the facilities, if you don't mind.'

'Oh absolutely, be my guest,' said Ben, then went bright red and scurried for the stairs.

'Luke's a heck of a teacher,' said Jemma, once the coast was clear.

'Never mind that,' said Em. 'I'm going into the staff bathroom now in case Ben's listening.' She stomped through to the back room, and Jemma followed on tiptoe. The key was in the stockroom door. 'Are you sure you won't go up to Raphael's flat?'

'I can't risk it till Ben leaves. What if he hears me moving overhead?'

'OK.' Em moved towards the bathroom.

'Wait— If you need to contact me, I'm using my secret phone. I've left the other one in my flat. Give Maddy the number, too, but don't use it unless you absolutely have to.

I don't want the police coming after you.'

Em gave her a quick, tight hug. 'Good luck,' she whispered, and went into the staff toilet.

Gently, Jemma eased the key round in the lock. It made a low click, and she exhaled her pent-up breath. She turned the handle, and went in.

The room was dark, and she didn't dare switch the light on. *What do I do now? Oh, this is terrible.* Her stomach rumbled, and she realised that she had forgotten to pack any food or a drink. *You'll have to manage*, she told herself sternly. *You've had a couple of cinnamon rolls; you won't starve.*

She heard the toilet flush, followed by footsteps and the creak of the great oak door, and the faint sound of talking. Then her blood froze at a rap on the shop door. *It can't be —*

Beneath her, the talking stopped. 'Should we answer that?' said Ben.

'Let's see if they knock again,' said Em. 'They may not have read your notice. That was a great idea, by the way.'

They're here, and they'll find me. Jemma looked around wildly for help. *The cupboard under the sink! There's always something there.*

She left the stockroom, ran to the cupboard and threw it open. Inside, on top of J-cloths, bottles of washing-up liquid and the first-aid kit, was a box labelled *Self-Inflating Dinghy*. She stared at it in wonder, then grabbed it and retreated to the stockroom. This time, she took the key and locked the door behind her.

The knocking resumed, more insistent this time. Ben

heaved a huge sigh. 'I suppose I shall have to send them away.'

Jemma took the dinghy out of the box. It was bright orange, with a red cord from which dangled a label. *Pull to inflate*, it said.

Jemma frowned at it: *How can I use this?* Then she remembered the trapdoor that had appeared in the stockroom, once upon a time. 'That wasn't real,' she muttered. 'Raphael magicked that up. Raphael and Folio.'

Then she looked at her bracelet. Even in the darkness, the colours of the stones were visible, twinkling purple and deep yellow. She gave it three quick turns, for luck, then went to the back of the stockroom and lifted the carpet, the underlay, and finally, the shabby linoleum. She fully expected the usual unbroken floorboards, and gasped as she saw first the corner, then the whole trapdoor, iron ring and all. She wrenched it open, got her rucksack, and switched on her phone torch. A set of stone steps were illuminated. She tucked the dinghy under one arm and began to descend.

Whoever was outside was banging on the door. Feet hurried past, too heavy to be Em's. 'What's wrong with this door?' Ben muttered.

'Open up! Police!' a voice shouted. 'Don't make us break the door down.' Jemma held her breath, frozen to the spot. *Thank heavens I locked the stockroom door.*

The shop bell jangled as the door opened suddenly. 'Oh, hello,' said Ben, and she could imagine his nervous face. 'How may I help you, officers?'

'We have a warrant for the arrest of a certain Jemma

James,' said a gruff voice. 'We have just seen a person answering to her description entering your premises. Can we take a look around, please?'

'I think you're mistaken,' said Ben, but Jemma heard heavy boots coming into the shop. She seized the inner ring of the trapdoor and pulled it shut. *Please vanish*, she willed it. Above her, the floor coverings flopped into place.

Apart from the beam of her torch, it was pitch black. She heard a faint rushing noise. *The underground river...* She remembered Damon's cries when it had tried to sweep him away, and trembled.

'Sarge, this door's locked,' someone shouted, their voice muffled slightly by the trapdoor.

'Get the Enforcer on it!'

That was enough to make Jemma hurry. The rushing was louder now. Another step, and another, and another. Water lapped below.

Boom! The whole shop shook.

Jemma held the limp dinghy in front of her and pulled the red cord. The dinghy ballooned immediately. Jemma lost her grip, and it bounced down the steps and smacked onto the water. 'No!' she wailed.

'Someone's in there!' the voice shouted.

Boom!

Her hand trembling, Jemma shone her torch on the place where the steps met the water. She had expected the dinghy to be gone, yet it bobbed in place. She hurried to it and put one foot in, bracing herself for an alarming lurch, but it stayed steady. 'I don't understand,' she whispered, 'but thank you.' She got into the dinghy, sat down, and put her rucksack at her feet.

Boom! Wood splintered.

'One more!' someone bellowed.

Boom! The door swung open and banged against the wall.

The dinghy rose, then moved slowly forward. *We're moving. Oh heck, we're moving! Where are we going?* She remembered she was a terrible sailor, and put her head between her knees to combat seasickness. A gentle breeze ruffled a few strands of hair that had escaped from the hat.

'It'll start lurching in a minute,' she muttered. 'It'll pitch, and toss, and spin round, and it'll be awful.' She looked for a handle or a rope to clutch, but the sides of the dinghy were smooth and unforgiving. *I should switch off the torch. I'm wasting the battery, and I forgot my charger.* She fumbled at the buttons, and swallowed as she was plunged into darkness.

'I'm scared,' she whispered.

Then an arm slid around her middle, and she caught her breath. No, not an arm; it was too thin to be an arm. Too curved to be an arm. Too flexible to be an arm. She reached a tentative hand down and encountered smooth, firm, damp skin punctuated by . . . suckers?

The octopus?

Another tentacle moved across her lap, holding her gently but securely, like a sort of seatbelt. Carefully, she patted it, and the skin pulsed at her touch.

The breeze quickened, the dinghy speeded up – or was it the octopus speeding up? – and the water churned beneath them.

Chapter 14

Time passed . . . oddly. Occasionally Jemma flashed her torch around, but she never saw more than a glimpse of a brick archway, or a rugged rock face. *Where are we going? Where am I?* Then again, if she didn't know where she was, presumably the police didn't either. Somewhere under London was her best guess. *I should have checked when we started*, she thought. But it was hard to have presence of mind or foresight when embarking on a bizarre underground journey steered by an octopus.

She remembered Alice's fall down the rabbit hole, and wondered whether she would encounter shelves, cupboards, and a jar of orange marmalade on her travels, but her surroundings remained disappointingly empty. Or reassuringly empty, depending on your view. Once she called out 'Hello?' to see if anyone else was travelling by underground river, but the sound bounced and echoed so persistently that she put her hands over her ears and resolved not to do that again.

At one point the waterway dipped, and Jemma heard

rushing overhead that drowned out the water she was travelling by. *Are we going under another river? Perhaps it's the Thames. In that case, we must be going south. Mustn't we?*

A short while later, the dinghy came to a halt beside a dim red light. Something pale and rectangular glimmered near it, but Jemma couldn't make it out. She used her torch, and found it was a sign with a pointing hand, on which was written *The Earl's Sluice*. *I'm not sure how I feel about that*, she thought, but at that moment the red light glimmered green, and they were off.

The waterway wound silently through more rock. *Where will it come out? It will, won't it?*

You have to come out somewhere, she told herself, though she wasn't at all sure that was the case.

And what do I do when I get there?

Her inner voice said nothing, and Jemma suspected it had executed a shrug. She sighed, and patted the octopus's tentacle again. *What a journey this is. I ought to be appreciating it. How many people get to travel an underground river by octopus?* She imagined reading an article about her experience, or watching a TV series: *Travels By Octopus*. Or a poster, like the ones for the Tube. *That would be something to look at while you wait for a train.* She visualised the underground rivers and the pipes of the Tube intertwining, and marvelled at the intricacy of the world below.

Then she saw light ahead. A pinprick at first, then growing. She strained her eyes to make out her location, but she was too far away. *At least it comes out somewhere,* she thought, and wrapped her arms around herself.

The light grew and grew until the dot was a circle, and the circle plainly the end of a tunnel. Beyond it buildings rose into the sky. *Still in London, then.*

The dinghy speeded up, as if the octopus wanted to get to the end of the journey, too. The rushing water grew louder and louder, and the dinghy rocked from side to side. Then it took off. Jemma gripped her octopus seatbelt, gritting her teeth, and prayed to no one in particular for a safe landing.

The dinghy smacked down, making a huge splash, and Jemma's feet were doused in icy water. 'Aargh!' she cried. But the octopus swam on.

Jemma narrowed her eyes against the light. The air was sharp and almost too fresh after the slightly stale, musty atmosphere of the tunnels. She was travelling on a wide river lined with tall, modern buildings, none of which she recognised. *This is the Thames, isn't it?* She tried to relax as she wondered how much further there was to go. She looked around her, conscious for the first time of the sunshine and the green trees on the banks of the river. *It's spring, and I never noticed.*

Then her phone rang. Jemma reached for it, perplexed. *How is it that half the time I can't get a signal in the middle of London, yet in the middle of the River Thames there's no problem whatsoever?* The display said *Mum*. She grimaced, and pressed *Answer*.

'Jemma, I've had such a funny call,' her mother said, without preamble. 'It was a man who said he was from the City of London police.'

'Did he give a name?'

'Inspector someone. Platt, that was it. Anyway, he wanted to know if I'd seen you or spoken to you lately. Apparently he's keen to discuss an incident in a library.'

Jemma concentrated on keeping her breathing steady. 'What did you say, Mum?'

'Obviously I played dumb and said no, you hadn't been home for a while and apart from our usual weekly phone call and the odd text I hadn't heard from you particularly.' She paused. 'Do you think he was genuine?'

'I don't know,' said Jemma.

'Well, do you know anything about an incident at a library? He seemed very cagey. You aren't mixed up in anything, are you?'

A passing ship let out a loud honk.

'What was that? Where are you? That doesn't sound like the bookshop.'

'I'm, um, out of the office.'

'Clearly, but where? Why aren't you answering your other phone? I thought that was fixed and this was a backup.'

'Can I call you back? I can't talk right now.'

'Jemma, what's going—'

Jemma ended the call and shoved the phone in her rucksack. *Even if I knew where I was, Mum, I couldn't tell you.* And then she did know where she was, as she saw the park, the twin domes of the old Naval College, and the white wedding cake that was the Queen's House. 'Greenwich,' she whispered. 'The Meridian.'

I'm at the beginning of time.

***

The octopus veered towards a narrow stretch of pebbly sand, with stone steps leading up to the main river walk, and gently unwound its tentacles.

'Thank you,' said Jemma. She held out her hand, and after some hesitation the octopus offered her the end of a tentacle, which she shook. 'Perhaps we'll meet again.'

The octopus raised two tentacles in a sort of shrug then, with a shimmy, slid the dinghy into the water. Jemma just managed to stumble out before it bobbed away. She looked at her baseball boots, which were ankle-deep in water. *It could be a lot worse, I suppose*, she thought, and trudged to the steps.

Five minutes later she was sitting at the rear of a café, with a cup of searingly hot coffee and two rounds of buttered toast. She had paid in cash: using her card was too risky. The toast disappeared quickly, and she wondered how long she could survive on the five-pound note and change that she had left. *So much for a cash-free society. But what now? I ought to tell the others that I'm safe.* She sent a quick text to Em: *Got out safe. Tell the others. J x*

Then she remembered, with a terrible rush of guilt, that Carl had no idea what was going on. *What if the police contact him? What on earth will he think?* She remembered her own musings on her guilt, and shivered.

This is hard to explain but I've left the bookshop for a while. I hope things will be OK, but I don't know. It's probably best you don't contact me yet. I'll be in touch, I hope. J x

She had sent the text before she realised she hadn't put *I love you*, *Love*, or anything but the *x* she ended most texts with. *Too late now. But why didn't I?* She stared at the phone. *Too much on my mind, I suppose.* She drank some still-scalding coffee, and decided to leave it at that.

Then her phone rang. *I told him not to contact me!* she thought, with a touch of irritation.

But the display didn't show Carl's name. It showed the name of someone she had never expected to hear from again.

Jasper Bantam.

Jemma stared at the phone as it rang. *Why are you ringing now, after weeks of ignoring me?* She was tempted to reject the call; what help could Jasper be?

Then the penny dropped as to exactly how much help he could be, and she pressed *Answer*.

'Jemma, I'm worried about you,' Jasper said. To be fair, he did sound worried. *I'm worried about me, too.*

'So worried that you've been avoiding me for weeks?'

'I can explain,' said Jasper. 'But things are very odd, and I had to make sure you were all right. *Are* you?'

'I guess that depends on how you define all right,' said Jemma. 'I haven't been arrested yet today, so that's good.'

'Yes, I wondered about that,' said Jasper. 'I've had a visit from a couple of police officers. They asked if I'd seen you or spoken with you recently. Of course, I said no.'

For the first time, Jemma felt relieved that Jasper had blanked her so comprehensively. 'Good. What did they want?'

'They said you'd been accused of assaulting someone and they were gathering evidence on other incidents. I said that was very out of character. Then they mentioned it had taken place in the British Library, and I realised who it must be. I had to phone you. *She's* why I've been incommunicado.'

'Drusilla?'

'That's right. After the – the incident at the London Library, the one Dr Nash sorted out, she threatened me, and the library. She said that was just the beginning, and that things would get a whole lot worse unless I cooperated.'

Jemma's stomach shifted unpleasantly. 'What did she ask you to do?'

'She asked me to find out what was going on. Where Raphael was, what you were doing.' He paused, as if gathering himself. 'When I invited you to the hotel for a cup of tea, I'm afraid I was trying to obtain information. But when you dashed off to the knowledge emergency at the Maughan Library and got hurt, I knew I couldn't do it. I couldn't betray you. So I didn't tell Drusilla anything, and I ghosted you.' Another pause. 'I'm sorry,' he muttered.

'I understand,' Jemma said automatically. Her head was in a whirl. *So Drusilla is definitely out to get us*, she thought wearily. 'Did she say what her plans were?'

'Not in so many words,' said Jasper. 'I mean, it's not one of those films where the villain says they'll tell you everything before they kill you, and then you escape. I wish life *was* like that; it would be a lot easier. But she did say that she didn't need the Guild any more as she had formed a powerful new partnership, and that if I had any sense I'd take her side, because the Keepers' Guild had no chance.'

'What did you say?'

'I said I'd think about it.'

Jemma could imagine him in meeting mode, making no promises, only vague noises. 'You didn't,' she said.

'Of course not. I wavered when she threatened the library, but libraries aren't just nice buildings with books in, are they? *People* make a library.'

'Yes,' said Jemma, 'they do.' She paused. 'Jasper, would you do something for me?'

'Of course,' said Jasper.

'Could you book somewhere for me to stay in Greenwich? I don't care what it's like so long as it's got a bed and Wi-Fi. I can't go home, not while the police are looking for me.'

'I can do that,' said Jasper. 'Anything else?'

Jemma bit her lip. 'Once you've booked it, can you order me a phone charger to be delivered there? I forgot mine, and I haven't enough money to buy one.' She turned her phone over and told him the model number.

'OK, got that. Do you need food?'

'Food would be nice,' said Jemma, feeling terribly guilty.

'I'll see what I can do.' He sounded brisk, and happy to be doing something practical. 'We can't let Drusilla win. Bye for now. And – I'm truly sorry.'

'I know—' But Jasper had already rung off.

Ten minutes later, when Jemma was contemplating the dregs of her coffee, her phone buzzed. The text was from an unknown number. *Have booked a room in a B&B for two nights, in the name Jodie Smith. Room available from 5pm. Will put address in separate message, just in case. Charger coming tomorrow, food arriving later. Use this number in future and delete messages once read. Jasper.*

Jemma felt ready to weep at his kindness. Instead, she went to the bathroom, used the facilities and had a quick wash. She was surprised that she appeared as usual in the bathroom mirror. *I'm not even the same person I was this morning. As for a year ago...* She remembered her former life, mired in spreadsheets, dashing to meetings, and spending too many evenings getting merry to forget about it. *Would I change back?* Then she grinned. *Probably not.* But for now, her job was to lie low.

She left the café and made for Greenwich Park. No one would expect her to be there, and perhaps a brisk walk would clear her head. Yet as she climbed the hill and paused to look out over the city, thoughts swirled around her brain in such a random manner that she couldn't make sense of them at all.

Chapter 15

Jemma woke the next morning feeling ready to face the day. When she had arrived the previous evening at the B&B Jasper had booked, she found not the modest bedroom she had expected but a separate flat, nicely furnished, with its own entrance. 'Come and go as you please,' the owner said, putting the key into her hand. 'If you need anything, I'm only upstairs. All I ask is that you don't throw any parties. Enjoy your stay.'

Jemma had expected to lie awake half the night worrying, but after she had eaten the pizza which Jasper had ordered for her – *how does he know I like pepperoni and mushrooms?* – and drunk a good strong cup of tea, she curled up in the big white bed, thought dimly that the iron bedstead looked as if it might be magical, and drifted off to sleep.

She got a nasty jolt in the morning when she realised no cats were on the bed, and why that was. Then she remembered she was safe, and the others were coming today. *Be careful*, she had texted. *Use cash whenever you can, and if anyone is following you, don't come here. I'll see you at 10.*

But on the dot of ten o'clock, the doorbell rang and there were Luke and Em, their faces a mixture of curiosity and relief. 'Come in,' said Jemma. 'I'll put the kettle on. Where's Maddy?'

'On guard,' said Luke. 'She's spending time with the cats and making sure Lennox and Ben don't get into the Friendly Bookshop or your flat, what with it being Sunday. And she sent this.' He dug a hand into the pocket of his black jeans and passed Jemma a small, tightly folded wad of banknotes. 'She says you can pay her back, plus overtime, when this is over.'

Jemma grinned. 'I will. Plus a pay rise.'

'We brought snacks,' said Em, waving a brown paper bag from which a cinnamony smell issued. 'And crisps and chocolate and Diet Coke. We weren't sure if you had money to eat.'

Jemma closed the door behind them and led the way to the kitchen. 'Jasper provided.'

'Jasper?' asked Luke. 'As in Bantam? I thought he was ignoring you.'

'He isn't now, and he told me why. It was to do with Drusilla.' As she found mugs and teabags, Jemma told them the story. 'She's been trying to spy on us for ages. It's just luck that Jasper's on our side.' *And maybe likes me*, she thought, but she kept that to herself.

'It's still pretty bad, though,' said Luke. 'I mean, Jasper didn't do what she wanted, but maybe someone else did.'

'Who else do I talk to?' asked Jemma. 'Apart from you

and Maddy, and reporting to Lennox, and Carl, who doesn't understand most of it anyway, who else is there?' The kettle switched itself off, and she made the tea. 'Anyway, let's get to work.'

'There's something I should tell you before we start,' said Luke, as they sat down at the small kitchen table. 'The police came to the Friendly Bookshop once they'd finished breaking into Burns Books, and they asked me for a statement. I said I didn't know where you were, which was completely true, but also that I was in the British Library when the incident happened. Obviously, I didn't say anything about the Guild or the magical stuff, but I did say that the woman who ran away had dropped something which gave off smoke and made a mess of the library floor. Hopefully that's done you some good.'

'Thanks, Luke,' said Jemma. 'Maybe they'll follow that up with the library staff. The difficulty is that we were alone in that room, so it's my word against hers.'

'It's so frustrating,' said Em. 'We know so much, and we can't use it.'

'Rules of the Guild,' said Jemma. 'Secrecy at all times. Anyway, let's get on. Drusilla told Jasper that she'd entered into a powerful new partnership.'

'Wouldn't that be River Logistics?' asked Em. 'They delivered all those red herrings, from what you said.' She frowned. 'I thought I saw one of their vans on the way here, but I could have been mistaken.'

'They were probably making a normal delivery,' said Jemma. 'You didn't see anything weird, did you? No one followed you from the van, or looked at you?'

'No,' said Em. 'no one was in the driver's seat, and while it was the right colour, there wasn't a logo on the van.'

'It wasn't even them, then,' said Luke. 'Oh, yeah, more good news. Your phone, the one you left behind, has been buzzing with messages from Guild members. Obviously we couldn't reply from your phone, but where we could we've texted and let them know that you haven't resigned and it's a misunderstanding. Everyone who replied is really happy about that.'

'How many people replied?' asked Jemma.

Luke made a face as he considered. 'Maybe two-thirds.'

'That's something – although maybe the others are cross that I might not be gone for good.'

'That's it, Jemma, look on the bright side,' said Em. 'Less than twenty-four hours ago you were running from the police.'

'There is that,' Jemma admitted, with a grin. 'What's happened with Burns Books? Is it still closed?'

'Ben said he'd pop down and check on the shop this morning,' said Em. 'I suggested he open up, actually; it'll keep him occupied. If he's busy, he isn't asking awkward questions or bothering me.' She looked rueful, and Jemma suspected she was finding her ability to cast glamour rather a double-edged sword.

'How terrible to be so attractive,' she said, laughing. 'Anyway, let's see what else we can find out about River Logistics.'

But as before, there was little to find. 'There must be something,' said Jemma, leaning on the table and putting her head in her hands. 'Either the company is beyond reproach, or very good at hiding things.'

'It's suspicious that there's so little online,' said Em. 'I've checked for mentions of the company on social media and Google. Even on sites like Glassdoor there isn't a bad word. Indeed, barely a word about them at all.'

'See?' said Jemma. 'It's odd.'

'Maybe it isn't them,' said Luke. 'Maybe that's the biggest red herring. Maybe Drusilla used the company to send us on the wrong track.'

'We need more tea,' said Jemma, and picked up their mugs. She gave them a quick rinse, primed them with teabags, set the kettle going again, and opened the drawer for a teaspoon. She stared at the contents, then pulled out a corkscrew.

Em laughed. 'It's a bit early in the morning, Jemma,' she said. 'Even for me.'

'No, it isn't that,' said Jemma. She twisted the handle and watched the corkscrew rotate. 'What was it she said?'

'What did who say?' asked Em. 'Now you're talking in riddles.'

'Let me think…' Jemma carried on turning the handle and staring at the corkscrew. 'We were at her house, and she said something odd.'

Luke and Em exchanged glances.

'*I have coiled myself around London like a serpent,*' said Jemma. 'That's what Drusilla said to Raphael, more or less. Then she said he couldn't disentangle her if he tried.'

Em shivered. 'I remember. That was pretty creepy. I

assumed she was shooting her mouth off, though. You know, to psych you and Raphael out before the big battle.'

'I did, too,' said Jemma. 'I haven't thought of it until now. What if it wasn't just big talk? What if she was speaking the truth?'

'How could she wind her way around London?' said Em. 'She can't wrap her arms round the buildings or the streets like a massive octopus.'

Jemma opened her mouth to speak, then realised that mentioning her octopus ride to Greenwich was probably a very bad idea. 'Well no, obviously,' she said. 'Not openly. How else could Drusilla get her paws on London?' She remembered the exceptionally dull meeting they had sat through at the headquarters of DZD Holdings, Drusilla's company, and tried to remember what had been discussed. Most of it had been time-wasting, designed to conceal their plan to demolish Burns Books behind their commission to build an underground transport hub—

'*Underground*,' she said. 'Drusilla's company specialised in underground things: basements and reinforcements. They've probably spent more time underground than above it. Who knows what they've done while they've been down there.'

'And River Logistics' headquarters is built at the source of an underground river,' said Luke. 'I thought Maddy was clutching at straws when she told me, but now...' He ran his hands through his hair and looked at the others with wide pale-green eyes. 'It's starting to make sense. Horrible sense. They're going to attack London from below.'

'The Mithraeum tried to warn us,' said Jemma. 'That's

underground, too. Somehow, rumours spread that far.' Her mouth was dry as she swallowed. 'This is terrible.'

Em got up and put an arm round her. 'It is terrible, but we must stay strong. I'll make tea, we'll have another cinnamon roll, and then we'll work out what to do.' She led Jemma back to the kitchen table and gently sat her down.

Luke's phone buzzed. He read the message and smiled. 'We'll need an extra cup: Maddy's coming.' He read out the message. *'Cats happy and all quiet so heading over. Waiting for DLR to Greenwich. See you soon x'*

'I hope she's being careful,' said Jemma.

'Of course she is,' said Luke. 'We were planning it last night. Don't you worry, Maddy can look after herself.'

Em brought more tea and Jemma checked the time. 'I suppose we should think about lunch.'

Luke pulled a Tupperware container from his bag. 'I'll eat separately.'

'Fine by me,' said Jemma, making a face. 'We'll decide what to eat when Maddy arrives. How are the trains running?'

'Fine,' said Em. 'No maintenance works, no lines closed.'

A few minutes later, the doorbell rang. Jemma got up and reached for the intercom. 'Wait,' said Em, and took the receiver from her. 'Just in case it's someone else. Hello?'

'It's me,' said Maddy's voice.

'That was quick! Everything OK?'

'Yes,' said Maddy, 'fine.'

'I'll go,' said Jemma. She went into the tiny hall and

peered through the spyhole in the front door. There was Maddy, looking anxious. *She's probably been worrying the whole way.* She opened the door wide. 'Come on in, we're all here.'

'Yes, we are,' said Lennox, stepping out from behind the hedge and seizing Maddy's arm. He pushed past Jemma, who was frozen with shock, and into the flat. 'Where are they? Ah, sitting round a table with a cup of tea. Almost as if you were working in my bookshop.'

'It isn't your bookshop,' said Jemma.

'I'm sorry,' said Maddy, her expression anguished. 'I never knew he was there until he grabbed me as I rang the bell. I'd have screamed but – I couldn't. It was as if he was controlling me.'

'You scumbag,' said Jemma, scowling at Lennox, who responded with a smug look that made her long to punch him. 'What do you want?'

'I don't want anything,' said Lennox, dropping Maddy's arm and spreading his hands. 'I've come to give you some news. You were on probation anyway, Jemma, but I regret to inform you that due to your unpredictable, unacceptable behaviour, ranging from mere incompetence to causing public disorder and bringing the good name of the shop into disrepute, you are fired.'

'I already resigned,' said Jemma.

'However, thanks to Raphael's foolish indulgence, you still retained membership of the Keepers' Guild and management of the Friendly Bookshop,' said Lennox. 'Given your mismanagement of that enterprise, I am taking back the management of that shop. And as your job at the shop includes accommodation, you had better clear yourself out before you're thrown out.'

'You can't do this,' said Jemma. 'You can't fire me.'

'I just did,' said Lennox. He took out his phone and showed Jemma a picture: a *WANTED* poster, with her face staring out of it. *I look like a criminal.* 'You may as well give up, Jemma. You can't win. We won't let you.' He dialled a number, and when the call connected, a mocking smile spread over his face. 'I've found her, Inspector.'

Chapter 16

Rage swept over Jemma like a breaking wave. 'How dare you,' she said. 'You know the truth, and you don't care.'

'No, I don't,' said Lennox, muffling the phone. 'However well-meaning your motives, Jemma, you're a danger to the Guild, and I want you gone.' He spoke into the phone. 'Yes, here is the address.' He moved to block the exit to the hallway. 'Not so fast, my dear.'

Breathing hard, Jemma held out her left hand, and her bracelet sparkled under the kitchen spotlights. She took a step forward. 'I'm warning you.' *I hope this works.*

Lennox smirked and drew himself up to his full height. 'There's no hurry, Inspector,' he said into the phone.

Jemma took another step forward, and the smirk vanished. He looked as if he were resisting a high wind.

'Move aside,' said Jemma.

'No,' Lennox replied, through clenched teeth. Jemma moved forward again, and he took a step back. 'You'll regret this, Jemma.'

'I don't care.' Jemma walked forward until Lennox was

squashed into a corner of the little hallway. Continuing to focus on him, she spoke. 'Everyone, get your things. We're leaving.'

'You won't escape,' said Lennox. 'The police are on their way. They know your approximate location already.' He glared at her. 'I'm not the only person tracking you.'

Behind her, Luke, Maddy and Em left the kitchen, laden with bags. 'Come on, Jemma,' Em murmured in her ear. 'The police are on their way.'

'When the police find you and lock you up, I hope they throw away the key,' said Lennox, all his bonhomie gone.

'Oh yes, the key,' said Jemma. 'What a good idea. Everybody out.' She heard the creak of the door, followed by the others' footsteps, and backed onto the doormat. 'Don't worry, Lennox, I'm sure the police won't be long. Don't make a mess.' Carefully, her left hand still outstretched to ward him off, she negotiated the step, closed the door, and locked it. 'I'm posting the key in the upstairs mailbox,' she called. 'You can tell the police that when they come.'

Em took her hand and pulled her away from the door. 'Run!' she hissed.

'No, don't run,' said Luke. 'Come this way.' He led them through a selection of side streets, alleys and passageways until they emerged on a main road, beside St Alfege Church.

'I didn't know you knew the area,' Maddy said, gazing at him in admiration as they tried not to hurry.

'I know most of the back ways of London,' said Luke. 'When you're a vampire trying to keep out of trouble, you get used to sneaking around and you pick up all the tricks. Kind of like the Knowledge for cabbies.'

'What now?' said Em, looking about her. 'The station?'

'Not yet,' said Luke. 'The police will have our descriptions, for sure. We must work on that.' He pointed at a shop with a large picture window, displaying mannequins in miniskirts and flapper dresses.

'Vintage clothing?' said Em, looking sceptical.

'Do you have a better idea?' He waited for perhaps half a second. 'In we go.'

Inside the shop, Em eyed Jemma critically, then selected a long print dress and a denim jacket from the rails. 'Try those,' she said. 'I'll find a bag and some other bits.' Jemma took them and retreated behind the curtain of a makeshift dressing room in the corner. Emotions jostled in her head: amazement at what she had done, relief that they had escaped, steely resolve to find and deal with Drusilla, burning-hot anger at Lennox, and, even sharper, shame that she was wanted by the police. She slipped into the dress and jacket, and peeped round the curtain.

'That's good,' said Em. 'Take off that hat and put this on.' She handed Jemma a bobbed dark-brown wig. 'Maddy's getting changed too, so it isn't just you.'

'What about you and Luke?'

'We'll manage. Pop the wig on.'

Jemma did as she was told, inspecting herself in the long mirror as she tucked her hair into the wig. Astonishingly, it fitted, though it didn't particularly suit her. *That's the least of your problems*, she told herself.

Em grinned when she pulled the curtain aside again.

'That's brilliant. We'll take it,' she called to the shop assistant. 'Now come here, and close your eyes,' she said, holding up an eyeliner pencil. Jemma submitted to what felt like a ridiculous amount of eyeliner, not to mention having her eyebrows drawn over, but when she dared to face the mirror, the effect was pretty good.

The curtain of the other fitting room rattled back and Maddy showed herself. She was wearing jeans and a Breton top, and her straight dark hair had become a blonde bubble perm that stood out round her head.

'Wow,' said Jemma. 'I would have walked straight past you.'

Maddy let out a nervous giggle. 'You too.'

'You both look great,' said Luke. 'And different, which is the main thing, but we must get moving. Could you do the honours, Jemma?' He glanced at the shop counter, and Jemma took the wad of cash from her jeans pocket.

'What now?' she asked, once she had paid the bill, which was much less than she had feared.

'Maddy and I turn left; you and Em turn right. We can't stay together,' he said, to Jemma's imploring gaze. 'The police will be searching for a group of four. We can meet later somewhere else.'

'Somewhere else?' Jemma's heart sank. Only that morning she had felt as if they were on the brink of sorting out the whole sorry mess. She had had a place to stay, a charger for her phone, money, and friends to help her. Now she was on the run again – and they were caught up in it too.

'I can't do this,' she muttered.

'Of course you can,' said Luke. 'Look at what you just did. You stopped Lennox in his tracks.'

'That wasn't me, was it?' Jemma said sadly, shaking her wrist. 'It was the bracelet Raphael gave me. Maybe you should leave me to it; I don't want you to get into trouble too. I mean, you're probably already in trouble for helping me—'

'So we may as well carry on,' said Em. 'The police will catch us if we hang around in Greenwich much longer. For all we know, they're letting Lennox out right now. If we delay any longer, we could all be in danger.'

'OK,' said Jemma. She took a deep, shivering breath. 'OK. What do we do?'

'The first thing is to work out where and when we'll meet,' said Luke. 'It can't be anywhere obvious, and we should stay off the Tube and the DLR. Lennox trailed Maddy, so he knows she came that way. The police could watch the CCTV and see where we are. Taxis are out, too: they might be able to trace the driver. So that leaves trains, which I'm not sure about for the same reasons, and that's it.'

'No it isn't,' said Jemma. 'You've forgotten the river.'

Luke raised an eyebrow. 'Is that wise?'

'I'm not sure, but it's different. To be honest,' she said slowly, 'I think I was tracked on my journey here, because part of it was by underground river, but the Thames would be safe. River Logistics can't possibly monitor all of it.'

She looked at the others to gauge their opinions and found them staring at her.

'You came by underground river?' said Em.

'Yes. I found a dinghy in the cupboard under the sink at Burns Books.' Jemma decided that was more than enough information.

'Oh well, if you found a *dinghy*.' Em flung her hands wide. 'OK, we'll take the river bus. I assume it goes from the pier. Where shall we meet? Any ideas?'

'No landmarks,' said Luke. 'Not the clock at Waterloo Station, or Nelson's Column, or anywhere near the bookshops.'

'Um, what about Docklands?' said Jemma. 'There must be a river-bus stop, and they won't expect us to go there. None of us have any links to it.'

'That's true,' said Luke. 'The only downside is that I don't know it well. Bit modern for me.'

'It's quite touristy in parts,' said Jemma. 'There are lots of cafés and restaurants. We could go to somewhere like Canary Wharf and find a coffee shop.'

'OK, let's do that,' said Maddy. 'But I want to go now.' She was shifting from foot to foot. *It's so odd seeing her in jeans*, thought Jemma. *She's probably thinking the same about me in this dress.*

'Right,' said Luke. 'You two go first, and Maddy and I will find another way to get to Docklands. Text us when you're settled somewhere.' He glanced at Jemma. 'Are you sure you're OK?'

'Not really,' said Jemma, in a low voice. 'I'm just keeping going. I can't even get hold of Raphael. I texted him yesterday and this morning, and nothing. Maybe he's given up on me.'

'I'm sure that isn't it,' said Maddy, rubbing her arm.

'Maybe he's angry at what's happened to the bookshops—'

'Nothing's happened to the bookshops,' said Maddy. 'Lennox was lurking outside the Friendly Bookshop this morning. I made sure the door was locked; that was all I could do. I heard a key in the lock and went into the back room because I couldn't bear to see him smirking at me when he came in, but he never did. And when I returned to the main shop, Luna and two of the kittens – the tuxedo one and the black one – were sitting in a row by the door.'

'Oh, good cats!' cried Jemma. 'But where were the others?'

'Probably at Burns Books, keeping him out of there,' said Luke, with a grin.

'I do hope so,' said Jemma. Then her face fell. 'How will they manage for food?'

'I left plenty in the back room,' said Maddy. 'The window's slightly open, and I'm sure Luna can fetch Folio and co if they don't work it out for themselves.'

'That's a relief,' said Jemma. She heaved a sigh. 'We have to do this, don't we?' She looked at the others for approval.

'Yes,' said Em. 'We do.' She took Jemma's hand and towed her to the door of the shop. 'I'll check the coast is clear, and then we're off. One, two, three—' And she pushed open the door of the shop.

Chapter 17

'All clear,' said Em. 'Come on.'

'Good luck,' whispered Luke and Maddy.

Jemma stepped into the street and glanced around nervously. No police officers, police cars, or mysterious dark-turquoise vans were visible, but she still felt uneasy. 'They could be in plain clothes,' she said.

'That's unlikely,' said Em. 'The cops who came to Burns Books were all in uniform. If we assume everybody is out to get us, we'll never get anywhere. Besides, you're in disguise.'

'You aren't,' Jemma shot back.

'Aren't I?'

Jemma looked at Em, or tried to. For some reason, her gaze kept slipping over her. She attempted to focus on one thing – Em's shiny hair, or her tote bag – but she couldn't do it. 'What are you up to?' she asked, narrowing her eyes.

'It's sort of anti-glamour,' said Em. 'Luke showed me on the way here. Instead of standing out, you sort of fade. I asked him about it after a couple of guys came into the bookshop with chocolates for me.' She grinned. 'It might be more useful than glamour.'

'Wish I could do it,' said Jemma. They walked down the street, making for the river.

'Will you be all right on the boat?' asked Em. 'Don't you get seasick? I remember that time work had the Christmas party on a boat. You spent most of the time clinging to the rail. And we weren't moving.'

'I'll manage,' said Jemma.

'I can't believe you escaped in a dinghy,' said Em. 'That must have been terrifying.'

'It was OK, once I got used to it.'

'You don't even like big boats.'

'It was fine,' said Jemma, testily. Em continued to look at her, and Jemma began to twitch with guilt. 'You'll probably find this hard to believe, but the secret trapdoor came back in the stockroom, and when I went down the steps with the dinghy, the octopus was there. It carried the dinghy and kept me safe, and swam with me until we landed at Greenwich.'

Em was so stunned that she forgot to de-glamourise herself. 'You *what?*'

Jemma shrugged. 'I said you'd find it hard to believe. But you know about the octopus, anyway, because of Damon.'

'So the octopus drove the getaway dinghy,' said Em. 'I've had some weird conversations, particularly at uni, but this has got to be the weirdest. So it didn't try to eat you?'

'No, it was friendly. We shook hands – well, tentacles – at the end. I can see you, by the way.'

'Darn.' Em narrowed her eyes and slid out of focus. 'Maybe you'll end up like one of those Disney princesses who gets the woodland animals to do her laundry.'

Jemma giggled. 'In London it would be pigeons and rats.' She looked in Em's general direction. 'Do you ever hear from Damon?'

'We stay in touch,' said Em. 'We went out for a long time; it would be weird not to. But he's still in Scotland and I'm here, so it wouldn't work.'

'Do you want it to?' Jemma had never understood what Em saw in Damon, with his shiny suits and his constant talk of doer-uppers and square footage, and when he had tried to swindle Raphael out of the bookshop, she had dismissed him as a bad lot.

'I know you two never got on,' said Em, 'but when he wasn't trying to impress people and it was just us, he was so nice to me. He was more like that in Scotland, but he kept banging on about that octopus and I couldn't stand it any more. I came back mostly to show him. And that worked, didn't it.' She gave Jemma a wry smile.

'You've slipped again,' said Jemma.

Em hastily blurred herself. 'It's harder to do when you're feeling stuff.'

'Aren't most things,' Jemma replied. They were at the Cutty Sark now, its masts towering over them. 'I can see a boat; we must be near the pier.'

'Yup,' said Em. 'Right, you're Helen and I'm, um, Jade, in case anyone's listening.'

'I thought you said there'd be no plain-clothes cops.'

'There's no harm in being careful,' said Em.

They reached the pier, consulted the timetable, and found that a boat bound for Canary Wharf was due to leave in five minutes. Em went to the kiosk to buy tickets, leaving Jemma fidgeting beside some wrought-iron railings.

That five minutes was the longest of Jemma's life. She could think of nothing to talk about, and in any case, having got tickets, Em was busy on her phone. 'I've told the others we're leaving soon,' she said.

'Oh, OK.' A message flashed up on Em's phone and she replied, then put the phone in her pocket. 'We should probably keep messages to a minimum.'

'I am doing,' said Em, and inspected the river. 'I can see it coming.' A long, low black and white boat which reminded Jemma of a torpedo was gliding towards them.

They boarded the boat and went inside. Despite the beige leather seats, Jemma gritted her teeth for what she suspected would be an uncomfortable journey.

'Relax,' said Em. 'You're all tense. I know you don't like boats, but it's only a quarter of an hour or so.'

Jemma nodded, not trusting herself to speak. She sat looking straight ahead and gripping the armrests, worried that if she made eye contact with any of the other passengers one of them might recognise her and alert the transport police.

She checked the time: one minute until the boat was due to leave. *Once we pull away, I'm safe.* She fiddled with the bracelet on her left wrist, turning it and watching the stones gleam. Then she heard a faint change in the note of the engine, and when she looked up, the boat was moving.

She closed her eyes, leaned back in her seat, and exhaled.

'That wasn't so bad, was it?' said Em.

'Not yet,' Jemma replied. In her head she was repeating the mantra *I've travelled along an underground river in a dinghy and I can do this*, over and over again.

She started violently when Em nudged her. 'It's our stop next,' she said. 'Canary Wharf. See? I told you it would be a breeze.'

'Yeah,' said Jemma, trying to keep the sarcasm out of her voice. She wouldn't have been surprised to find a crop of grey hairs when she removed her wig later.

She braced herself to be met by a squadron of police officers, but they disembarked without incident. 'Where to?' said Em. 'I don't know my way around.'

'You mean Damon didn't take you to any flash Docklands parties?' Em raised her eyebrows. 'Sorry.' She thought for a moment. 'We'll go this way. There's a café tucked away that isn't too expensive.' She turned left and took Em along a main road, then down a side street, into an alley, then left again. On the corner was a small, plain café called Sue's.

'How do you know this place?' asked Em. 'Is your bracelet showing you the way?' She glanced at it doubtfully. 'If so, it's excellent at multitasking.'

'I'll tell you inside,' said Jemma, 'over lunch.'

They found a booth near the back, and after some deliberation, Jemma went to the counter to order tea for two, two cheese toasties, and a chocolate brownie to share. Sue, the owner and, as far as Jemma knew, sole staff member, gazed at her with a quizzical expression, as if trying to place her, but she took the order with a smile, and Jemma heaved an inner sigh of relief.

'The tea's coming, and the toasties will be ready in five minutes,' she said, sliding into the booth.

'Great,' said Em, putting her phone away. 'Now tell me how you know this place.'

Jemma fished cutlery and a paper napkin from the pot on the table. 'Do you really want me to?'

'Yeah, or I wouldn't ask.' Em had resumed her normal appearance, presumably to save energy; Jemma remembered how Luke had looked fatigued following a full display of casting glamour.

She picked at her napkin. 'When I worked in the city,' she said eventually, 'I used to dream of having a flash job in Docklands, on the top floor of one of the skyscrapers. Sometimes, at weekends, I used to come here, wander, and daydream. I imagined what it would be like to have a corner office, and send my PA out for my lunch, and go to champagne receptions after work.' She snorted. 'I was bankrupting myself buying lunch from the places the traders went to, so I started coming here instead.' She tossed the napkin on the table. 'I'd never have made it, anyway. I don't know why I'm telling you this, but I want to be honest with you.' *In case a time comes when we can't speak to each other again.*

Em bit her lip. 'In that case, there's something I should tell you. But you have to promise not to tell anyone, ever. Not Carl, or Raphael, or anyone.'

Jemma's eyes widened. 'Go on,' she said, quietly.

'I know why you got made redundant,' said Em. 'Well,

you were sacked, let's face it.'

'Thanks for that; I didn't need reminding.' Even now, it hurt. 'What did I do?'

'Remember when you had a bee in your bonnet over corporate social responsibility and green issues, and you wrote a report in your spare time, with a list of recommendations?'

'Vaguely,' said Jemma. 'I was enthusiastic about a lot of things, wasn't I?'

'Yes, you were,' said Em. 'And when your boss Phoebe read that report, she told you she couldn't fault it. Remember? You were so pleased.'

'I was.' That felt like another life now. 'Is this going somewhere?'

'Yeah, I'm afraid so. You made lots of recommendations on green energy and going carbon neutral, and proved the organisation would save money. The shareholders would have loved it. But what you didn't know – and neither did I, at the time – was that Phoebe's brother's company had the energy contract for the organisation's buildings, and they didn't do green energy. He'd have lost a chunk of business overnight.'

'So Phoebe got rid of me and buried the report,' said Jemma.

A crease formed between Em's eyebrows. 'You're taking this well.'

Jemma shrugged. 'I suppose I am.' Sue arrived with their tea, then departed with a faint frown on her face.

I ought to feel more, Jemma thought, as she poured tea for both of them. *I ought to be furious with Phoebe, or pleased that it wasn't my fault. I could take her to a tribunal, if Em says it's OK.* But instead she felt blank. Blank and curiously light, as if something she hadn't even known she was carrying had gone.

Em's phone buzzed and she dived into her bag. She read the message, then put the phone back.

'Who was that?' asked Jemma. 'Was it Luke or Maddy?'

'No,' said Em, but her gaze moved past Jemma to the door.

'Em, what's going on?'

'Nothing's going on,' said Em, but her eyes wouldn't meet Jemma's.

'Then who texted you?' The door creaked behind her. Images flashed through her mind: Em texting before they got on the boat; Em putting her phone away as she came back from ordering lunch. She stared at Em, horrorstricken. 'Don't tell me that after all this, you've—'

Em's gaze moved past her again, and Jemma felt a hand on her shoulder. But instead of gripping her and pulling her to her feet, the hand turned her gently. Carl's expression was questioning at first, then relaxed into a huge grin. 'I found you,' he said, and gathered her into his arms.

Chapter 18

'I'm so glad to see you,' Jemma murmured into Carl's shoulder. She felt a sob welling up, and willed it back down. *If I spoil my eyeliner, Em'll kill me.* Then she remembered what she had just been thinking. 'I'm sorry, Em,' she quavered. 'For a moment I thought you'd set a trap.'

'I'm sorry,' said Em, quietly. 'I should have told you, but I was worried you'd say Carl couldn't come.'

'I would have come anyway,' said Carl. He released Jemma gently and scrutinised her. 'It's an interesting new look, I must say.'

'It's temporary,' said Jemma, firmly. 'You wouldn't believe how itchy this wig is.'

'Oh, I would,' said Carl. 'I wore enough dodgy wigs at drama school to last me a lifetime. Um, do you mind if I sit down?'

Jemma heard a throat clearing and whipped round to see Sue holding two plates. 'Your toasties.'

'Oh, thank you.' Jemma took the plates. 'Do you want

anything, Carl?'

'Um, a cup of tea and a bacon roll would be nice, thanks,' said Carl. He slid into the booth and Jemma squeezed in next to him.

'Right away,' said Sue, and scuttled off. *I couldn't have been more memorable if I tried,* thought Jemma, ruefully.

She reached for Carl's hand and squeezed it. 'How come you're here? What about the play?'

'The play's fine,' said Carl. 'The cast have settled into the new venue and they'll be OK without me for a few days at least. Even if they weren't, I'd still have come. I've been so worried; when I get your last message I didn't know what to do. I wanted to reply, but I thought that might make things worse for you. So I texted Em instead and she filled me in. I told Michael and Janina that a few days out would help me get a handle on finishing the next play, and took off.'

The door creaked again and she twisted round in the booth to see Luke – or a rough approximation of Luke – and Maddy. Maddy looked apprehensive, but when she saw Jemma she brightened, and gave her a little wave. As she did so, Luke resolved into his usual appearance. He seemed tired, but relieved. 'I'm glad we found you,' he said, coming over. 'I was starting to wonder whether this place existed. Everything's so shiny and new, even the refurbished buildings. It's quite off-putting.'

'How did you get here?' Em asked them. 'Did you take the river bus too?'

'No, we walked to North Greenwich then took the Jubilee line,' said Luke. 'Anyway, good to see you, Carl,' he said, shaking his hand. 'It's been a while.'

'Hasn't it,' said Carl. 'Although maybe I've left one drama and walked into another. What's the latest? Em told me someone's spreading rumours and they set the police on you. What's that about?'

In between bites of her cheese toastie and an occasional glance round to make sure Sue wasn't hovering, Jemma gave a brief account, helped by the others. 'We think Drusilla has partnered with River Logistics, as well as her own firm, DZD Holdings, and they'll attack London from below.'

'River Logistics, huh?'

Carl's bacon roll arrived, and Maddy ordered two decaf teas and a hummus salad wrap for herself. Carl put his bag on his knee and scrabbled within. Eventually, he held up a copy of the *Financial Times* and flicked through the pages with difficulty, given how full the booth was.

'Since when have you read the *Financial Times*?' asked Jemma.

'Since I grabbed a copy someone left on the Tube and used it to hide behind,' said Carl. 'Newspapers are great props.' He found the page he was looking for, folded the paper back on itself, and put it on the table. 'This is from yesterday.'

'*Going Postal*,' Jemma read aloud. '*River Logistics CEO announces dramatic new expansion plans.*' The photo showed a man in his mid-thirties, wearing a sharp suit and a satisfied smile. For some reason, she thought of Lennox.

River Logistics has always been a respected old

warhorse in the battle to control courier services in London, the article read. *Now that the Shore Brothers, long-time controllers of the company, have retired, Jordan Shore, family scion and new CEO, has big plans for the company. 'We can deliver more than just parcels,' he told our reporter. 'We've built a huge network over the years, and it's time for us to exploit it to the full.'*

'I don't like the sound of this,' she muttered, and read on.

The company's fleet of distinctive turquoise vans are a fairly common sight in the city, particularly in the Square Mile, but Mr Shore's ambitions spread far beyond transport of the four-wheeled variety. 'There used to be mail trains beneath London,' he said. 'Why not now? The Victorian postal network was known for its speed and reliability. We'll drive customer satisfaction up by digging down.'

When asked about the specifics of his plans, Mr Shore was, it is fair to say, guarded. However, he did hint that River Logistics might expand its services. 'We've seen what modern delivery companies can do,' he said. 'With some planning, we can change the landscape of London.'

Jemma put down the newspaper and took a deep draught of tea. 'That . . . is worrying.' She studied the others. Em was frowning. Maddy seemed ready to punch someone. Carl appeared rather confused, and Luke was gazing at her with a resigned expression. 'Why are you looking at me like that?' she asked him.

'Because I know what you're going to say next,' said Luke. He paused while Sue delivered their order.

'Go on then,' said Jemma, and he poured tea for himself and Maddy. She suspected he was playing for time.

'You'll suggest we go there,' he said. 'Do you want to go to the River Logistics HQ? Yes or no.'

'Yes, I do,' said Jemma. 'We've tried to find information about them and got nothing, so we must go to the horse's mouth.'

'And do what?' Luke countered. 'It's Sunday. They'll be closed.'

'Which makes today the best day to snoop around,' Jemma retorted. 'At least we'd be doing something, not running away. And Drusilla may be holed up there as well. We could kill two birds with one stone.'

'Yes, we can all get arrested for breaking and entering or stealing company information, or whatever they decide to throw at us,' said Luke.

'No one's doing anything until we've finished eating,' said Carl. He put an arm round Jemma and squeezed her gently. 'I know you don't want to sit and do nothing, Jemma, but we need to think this through.'

Jemma finished her toastie, chewing with vigour, then pushed the brownie towards Em. 'I've had enough,' she said.

Em cut the brownie in two, took half, and pushed the plate back. 'If you're going on an adventure, you might not get to eat for a while,' she said.

Jemma glanced at her. 'Aren't you going to argue with me?'

Em shrugged. 'What's the point? If you're determined to go, you'll go. But please don't go in feet first.'

'Me, feet first?' Jemma said. Then she sighed. 'OK. What I'll suggest, then, is that I scope out the building.'

'Just you?' said Luke. 'None of us should go anywhere alone: it's too risky. I'll come too. I can make myself inconspicuous, and if I have to get away quickly, I can always fly.'

'Are you sure you want to do that?' Jemma remembered the last expedition where Luke had assumed bat form. Due to the poor navigation of one of his bats, he had been rather weak and also slightly transparent for some time.

'I'm sure,' said Luke. He eyed Maddy's wrap, studied the menu for a while, then called towards the counter, 'Could I order a steak sandwich, please? As rare as you can make it.'

'Thanks,' said Jemma. She reached across the table and patted his arm, somewhat awkwardly. 'Once we've checked the place out, hopefully we can decide what to do next. I could pretend to be a journalist from the local newspaper, or maybe you could fly in through an open window and listen in on a meeting.'

'Let's just walk past it for now,' said Luke, 'if you don't mind.'

'While you're doing that,' said Carl, 'I'll check what's happening at Burns Books. That Ben hasn't met me, so I can pop in and see how things stand.' His face softened. 'Maybe I'll see the cats.' He smiled, then looked at Jemma. 'It'll take my mind off whatever you're doing,' he said sternly. 'Mind you take care of yourself. And Luke.'

'I will, I promise,' said Jemma. She finished her tea with a curious feeling brewing in her stomach: part anticipation, part apprehension. *What if something does happen to me?* Then she had an idea. She pulled out her phone, extracted a battered business card she had slipped into the back of the case, and dialled a number.

'Hawkins speaking,' said a gruff voice.

'Um, hello, this is Jemma James.'

A pause. 'It's been so nice and quiet with you on the run,' said Sergeant Hawkins. 'Apart from all the people trying to catch up with you, that is. What bombshell are you dropping on me this time? It's my day off, you know.'

'Sorry.' Jemma took a deep breath. 'I shouldn't do this,' she said, 'but I'm going to tell you the truth.'

***

'This beats the Tube any day,' said Luke, as the taxi drove along Shoreditch High Street.

Jemma didn't answer: she was looking for the church. Well, not so much the church as the buildings adjoining it. The taxi slowed and she saw, set back, a grey stone building more like a Greek temple than a church. 'I think this is it.' She checked the meter, and pulled out a couple of banknotes.

'Here we are,' said the cabbie. 'St Leonard's Church. What, actual folding money?' He sucked his teeth. 'I'm not sure I've got change.'

'Call it a tip,' said Jemma, and opened the door.

They walked down the short path to the church. When Jemma tried to glance at Luke, her eyes slid over him. *Probably wise*, she thought, and hoped that she too was sufficiently unrecognisable.

'What are we doing, exactly?' said Luke. 'I assume

we're not going to stand outside River Logistics and stare at it.'

Jemma swallowed. 'We should split up. I'll take a quick look at the building. If they are open – they'll still have parcels to deliver – you could go in and ask for directions. Tell them your phone's out of charge. They're a courier company; they'll know everywhere in London. I'd do it, but I don't want them to see me before I get into the building properly.'

'Fair point,' said Luke. He checked his phone. 'OK, this is the plan. According to my map, River Logistics is to our right. You go first, keep moving, and go round the block. I'll follow in a couple of minutes, looking confused, then I'll nip into the building and ask the way to a fast-food place. I'll meet you back here and we can compare notes.'

'OK.' Jemma huffed out a breath. 'That sounds good. Low risk.'

'That's the idea.' Luke managed a smile. 'Wish me luck.'

'Good luck.' They high-fived each other, and she set off down the church path.

Jemma wasn't sure what she had expected of the River Logistics headquarters, but this building wasn't it. It was a modest three storeys of metal, glass, and battered prefabricated panels. Only the sign, a breaking wave in vivid turquoise on white, was new or impressive. *The headquarters doesn't have to be fancy*, she thought, rather disappointed. Apart from anything else, the building seemed too modern to have any convenient dovecots or apertures for Luke to fly into. *The windows probably don't even open*, she thought in disgust. But the lights were on. Hope surged in her. *Luke can go inside—*

'Excuse me?' A young man stopped in front of her. He was holding a copy of *The Traveller's Guide to Secret London* and looking puzzled. 'Could you tell me where I might find the' – he peered at the book – 'the River Walbrook?'

'Most of it's underground,' said Jemma, 'but it's reputed to start at St Leonard's Church, which is there.' She turned to point it out. Then her arm was seized in a sharp grip, and she froze.

'Thank you so much.' The voice was higher, harsher, and very well bred, and when Jemma twisted round, the young man's features had sharpened into Drusilla's. Her blonde hair bristled, and her hazel eyes glowed like burning wood.

'Don't try to fight me,' she hissed. 'If you do, you'll regret it.' And she dragged Jemma into the building.

Chapter 19

Stay calm, Jemma told herself as Drusilla pulled her into the reception of River Logistics. *You wanted to get into the building, so you've got what you wanted. Kind of.* She hoped Luke had been close enough to see what happened, and that he would be sensible, keep away from the building, and contact someone who could help. She had given him Sergeant Hawkins's number, and he already had Raphael's. Privately, she thought Sergeant Hawkins would be a better bet.

To stop herself panicking, and divert herself from the fact that Drusilla was gripping her arm very forcefully and suffering no ill effects whatsoever, Jemma took note of her surroundings. The reception was marginally smarter than the exterior of the building, though the decor was approximately thirty years out of date. Before her was a steel and glass reception desk, behind which sat a woman in her twenties wearing a pussy-bow blouse, talking on the phone. She put it down hurriedly at their approach. 'Good afternoon, Ms Davenport.'

'Good afternoon,' Drusilla replied brusquely. 'Is Mr Shore available? I have something important to show him.' She gave Jemma a contemptuous look.

'Er, yes, he should be. Let me check.' She tapped at the keyboard of a smallish desktop computer. 'Yes, that should be fine. I'll ring down and let him know you're on your way.'

'Thank you,' said Drusilla. 'Now, lift or stairs?' She paused, considering. 'The lift will be safer. Less chance of you escaping.' She strode to the lift, dragging Jemma with her.

An awkward silence fell. 'So, have you enjoyed yourself?' Drusilla enquired, suddenly.

Jemma stared at her. 'Excuse me?'

'All this ducking and diving and going on the run. Was it enjoyable?'

Jemma wondered how to phrase a reply. 'It does rather cut into one's reading time,' she said, eventually.

Drusilla snorted, and was silent.

The lift arrived and Drusilla shoved her in. 'Keep your hands to yourself,' she instructed. A long, slightly gnarled finger, with its French-manicured nail, ran down the buttons and she pushed -1, next to which was written *Boardroom, Executive Offices, CEO*. There were two more floors beneath that: *Post Room and Offices*, and under that *River and Works*.

Carefully, Jemma slid her hand into her pocket and unlocked her phone. On the way over, she had set up a shortcut: if she could press the right part of the screen, she would call Sergeant Hawkins. She hoped he would have the sense not to speak when the call connected. She navigated to what she hoped was the correct area, and pressed it. 'What have you been doing lately, Drusilla?' she asked loudly, to mask any noise from her phone.

'Oh, this and that,' said Drusilla. 'Keeping tabs on you. Making arrangements.' She tapped the side of her nose. 'You'll find out in due course.'

The lift stopped abruptly with a clunk. 'With all that money, you'd think he would replace the lift, wouldn't you?' said Drusilla, as the door slid open. 'Now come along.' She pulled Jemma out of the lift and turned right: there was no other option.

Drusilla strode and Jemma stumbled down a corridor that was already much plusher than upstairs. The carpet was a thick, luxurious maroon, the overhead lighting designed to simulate daylight, and the walls were rich cream with wood panelling below. Eventually, they came to a door with a shiny brass plate: *Jordan Shore, CEO*. Drusilla rapped on it with her knuckle, and immediately a voice said, 'Enter.'

Jordan Shore's office didn't seem quite sure whether it was sleek and corporate or opulent Victorian. Steel and black leather chairs competed with a mahogany desk, and abstract paintings hung next to portraits in oils. Behind the desk sat the man whose photograph had been in the *Financial Times*, in an equally sharp suit and a silk tie with splashes of colour. And in the chair adjoining the desk sat Lennox Nash.

Jordan Shore stood up. 'Drusilla.'

Drusilla lifted her chin. 'Jordan. And Lennox. Always a

pleasure, though I didn't expect to see you here just yet.'

'Oh, I decided to drop in,' said Lennox airily. Then he looked at Jemma. 'I see you got changed, not that it's done you any good. You may as well take off that stupid wig.'

'With pleasure,' said Jemma, removing the dark-brown wig and shaking her hair out. 'I see the police made the mistake of releasing you after our little encounter earlier.' She would have loved to back him into a corner with her bracelet and wipe the smile off his face, but Drusilla was holding her wrist tightly and showed no sign of slackening her grip.

'You may have surprised me earlier,' said Lennox, 'but I think you'll agree that the tables have turned.'

'Haven't they just,' said Drusilla. 'Why don't you tell Jemma what you've been up to, Lennox?'

'Don't tell me you've been in on this from the start,' said Jemma. 'Raphael would have seen through you; I know he would.' Drusilla's grip tightened, and she had to grit her teeth not to cry out. Still, it was good that even the mention of Raphael's name angered Drusilla.

'Not at all,' said Lennox. 'If you hadn't made such an unholy mess, Jemma, perhaps I would have been content with things as they were. But no, you had to stick your nose into everything. A knowledge emergency here, an incident there, causing trouble as you always do.'

'The trouble was always there,' said Jemma. 'I merely brought it to light.'

Lennox glared at her. 'You made my position, and therefore that of the Guild, untenable. Is it any wonder that when Drusilla courted me, I listened?'

'I don't think I did court you,' observed Drusilla.

Lennox smirked. 'Oh, you did. You flattered me, you praised my abilities, you offered me a place at your right hand if I could deal with Jemma for you. And here she is, done up like a kipper.'

'No thanks to you,' retorted Jemma. A new thought struck her. 'I assume Armand Dupont doesn't know about your new allegiance?'

Lennox shrugged. 'What Dupont doesn't know won't hurt him.'

'This is fascinating,' said Jordan Shore. His voice was neutral, his accent not a London one – indeed, not identifiably from anywhere. Jemma suspected that had not always been the case. 'However, let's get to the point. I assume this young woman is the Jemma I've heard so much about.' He transferred his gaze to Drusilla. 'The one you've been trying to catch.'

'That is correct,' said Drusilla.

'Why have you brought her here, exactly? What am I supposed to do with her?'

Drusilla huffed out a sigh. 'I'd have thought that was obvious. But first I'd like her to suffer a little more. Lennox, why don't you tell Jemma exactly what you did to help bring her in.'

'You flatter me,' said Lennox. 'While it is true that I have never been particularly well disposed towards Jemma, most of my activities were merely designed to focus her on her rightful duties. Blocking her mobile phone during work hours, that sort of thing. My first inkling that it was time for a more significant change was when we inspected a book together.'

Jemma's mouth fell open. '*The Gentle Art Of Destruction*,' she said.

'That's it. A famous, or rather, an infamous book. It gravitated towards me, and it attracted me. I could handle it with relative ease, but when Jemma attempted to open it, the book disintegrated. I realised I was not the person I had believed I was – perhaps I never had been – and that led me to do some serious thinking.'

'I bet it did,' said Jemma, grimly. 'You told me my inexperience caused it.'

'Yes, I did,' said Lennox, inspecting his fingernails. 'It was then that I understood we were on opposing sides, though to all appearances we were on the same team. At last I knew why my dislike for you from the moment we met had been so strong. Can one fight one's own nature?' He shrugged, palms upwards. 'Or should one seek to express it?'

'So you tried to keep me out of the way,' said Jemma. 'The warning at the Mithraeum, the theft of the London Stone.'

'Oh yes,' said Jordan Shore. 'One of mine.' He seemed pleased to have something to contribute to the conversation.

But Jemma was still staring at Lennox, her lip curling as if he smelt of the sewers. 'And you set the police on me, of course. I've no doubt that you twisted what happened at the British Library and elsewhere, to try and put me in jail.'

'Well, you're so annoyingly persistent,' said Lennox.

'What's a man to do?' He smiled at Drusilla, but presumably received no encouragement, as he looked away quickly. 'Have you any idea how many opportunities I've sacrificed since I started in that blasted Keeper role? For that matter, do you know what I could have made if I'd gone into industry, instead of slogging my guts out for two hundred years messing about with books? Writing papers, writing lectures, sharing my hard-won knowledge with year after year of bored students, and for what? A pittance, that's what.'

'The path to knowledge is not always smooth,' said Drusilla, and Jemma was sure she detected a note of disapproval.

Lennox gave her a surprised glance. 'You were considerably more forthright on the subject the other day, Drusilla.'

'May I remind you that time is money,' said Jordan Shore. A small crease had developed between his eyebrows. 'Drusilla, by whatever means, you now have this – this Jemma person.'

'It's Jemma James,' Jemma said wearily. 'I don't know why people find it so hard to remember.'

Jordan Shore regarded her thoughtfully, swivelling in his chair like a brisk pendulum. 'Perhaps you aren't a memorable person, Jemma James.'

Lennox sniggered.

'I'm not sure why you're laughing,' said Jordan Shore. 'So far, you're all mouth and no trousers.'

Lennox's eyebrows shot up, but he remained silent.

Jordan Shore stopped swivelling, sat forward and spread

his hands on the desk. 'You've been a heap of trouble, Jemma James, which is why you actually are memorable. Organising rotas, orchestrating campaigns, stopping our agents, and frankly, being a nuisance.' His eyes, the colour of a grey Thames on a grey day, bored into Jemma's. 'That . . . interests me.'

At that moment, his desk phone buzzed. He lifted the receiver. 'Yes, Suzy?' He listened, his gaze lingering on each of them. 'No, that's fine. Go ahead.' He hung up, looked at the phone for a moment, then faced them. 'Where was I?'

'The amount of trouble Jemma has caused,' muttered Lennox.

'Oh yes. My question is, given how much trouble she can cause when she's against us, how much help could she be if she was with us?'

Jemma goggled at him, utterly taken aback. 'I'd rather die,' she spat.

'I'm sure that can be arranged,' snapped Lennox.

'Not so fast,' said Jordan Shore. 'Why don't you mull things over, Ms James. No need to give me an answer right now.'

An authoritative tap sounded at the door. 'Enter,' he said.

The door opened and Jemma let out a gasp. So did Lennox. Drusilla and the CEO remained silent.

Drusilla Davenport stalked into the room and glared with utter loathing at the Drusilla who still gripped Jemma's wrist. 'I thought as much.' She crossed the room, her hand outstretched like a claw. Jemma saw her wrist was bandaged.

The first Drusilla let go of Jemma. 'Don't do that,' she said, but her voice was already deepening.

'I knew something wasn't right,' said Lennox.

But all eyes were on the figure transforming before them. The blonde hair grew marginally shorter, and sandy. The figure changed shape, becoming taller and thinner. As it did, the designer suit became a plum velvet jacket and a pair of bottle-green corduroys, with a sky-blue shirt and a gold bow tie.

'Good afternoon, everyone,' said Raphael. 'I don't suppose there's any chance of a cup of tea?'

Chapter 20

'Well, isn't this nice,' said Drusilla, with a sneer. 'You've done me a favour, Raphael, bringing your protégée to visit us. And in the process, of course, weakening yourself.' She eyed Jemma. 'Take that bracelet off.'

'You must be joking,' said Jemma.

'Take it off, or Raphael here will be a pile of dust before you can say abracadabra.'

Jemma looked at Raphael for guidance. 'It's your choice,' he said. 'I have no doubt that she can do it. Or alternatively, her partner in crime over there.' He glanced at Jordan Shore. 'I never thought I'd be facing one of the Shore family in a situation like this.'

'They were too scared to use their abilities,' said Jordan Shore. 'They spent their lives hiding their power – and hiding me. Now that I run the show, I have no intention of letting my power go to waste.' Slowly, he extended a finger. 'I suggest you do as Drusilla says.'

Jemma put a trembling hand to the clasp of her bracelet, but as usual, it refused to obey her. 'Sorry,' she murmured, holding her wrist out to Raphael. 'Can you help?'

Silently, he unclasped the bracelet from Jemma's wrist and put it on the desk. Jemma swallowed the hard lump in her throat. She felt naked, vulnerable – and worse, she couldn't defend Raphael. A tear ran down her cheek.

'I hope you're satisfied,' Raphael said to Drusilla. 'It probably won't make much difference, in the scheme of things.'

'You should never have given her such a talisman in the first place,' said Lennox. 'All she has done is misuse it.'

'In your opinion,' said Raphael. 'And in my opinion, that's worth nothing. If you were a better man, you would be utterly ashamed of yourself.'

'Maybe I would,' said Lennox, showing no sign of remorse.

'Will you two stop bickering,' said Drusilla. 'Jordan, you know what to do. Frankly, I'm surprised she's still alive.'

'You didn't say anything about that,' said Jordan Shore. 'You just said you wanted to capture her. So it's time to hand over those rights you promised me.'

'Rights?' said Jemma. 'What rights?'

'It's none of your business,' said Drusilla. 'At least, it won't be in the very near future.'

The CEO leaned forward. 'I don't know if you're aware of Drusilla's company, DZD Holdings. They have done extensive underground work in the capital – often more than they were contracted for. That is useful to me.'

'*I have coiled myself around London like a serpent,*'

murmured Jemma. 'I knew it.' She looked at Jordan Shore. 'Are those works on the boundaries of wards in the City of London?'

The CEO waved a dismissive hand. 'That isn't important to me.'

So all those maps were a waste of time, thought Jemma. *The ward boundaries were just coincidence.* 'What do you plan to do with those rights?' she asked. *Keep him talking, and help may come.*

'Initially, I'll sit on them,' he said, leaning back in his chair and swivelling again. 'When the time is right, though, I intend to embark on what you might call a rewilding project.'

Jemma glanced at Drusilla. Her brow was slightly furrowed, as if this information was new to her, too. 'I don't understand.'

He chuckled. 'You wouldn't: it's on a quite unprecedented scale. I suppose you learnt about the Thames Barrier at school, in your geography lessons.'

'Um, briefly,' said Jemma. 'I didn't grow up in London.'

'In case you or anyone else has forgotten, it's intended to prevent the Thames from flooding London. If the rivers had their way, most of what we consider as London would be underwater.' He smiled at Jemma's horror. 'I won't do it all at once. I'll let the levels creep higher, obliterating a street here and a landmark there. Maybe pump up a few rivers at a time and see what happens.'

'Like you did with the Walbrook,' said Jemma.

'Precisely. That was a dry run to gauge the emergency

response. Or a wet run, maybe.' His smile broadened. 'You catch on fast.'

'Which landmarks do you have in mind?' said Drusilla, hoarsely.

Jordan Shore shrugged, spoiling the line of his suit. 'Whatever's in the way,' he replied. 'Obviously, central London would take the first hit. Fewer people live there, so it would be . . . unfortunate, rather than tragic.'

Drusilla's eyes bulged. 'You want to obliterate history,' she said. 'You want to wipe out what I've spent over a hundred years defending.'

'If you're that bothered, I could make a couple of exceptions,' said Jordan Shore. 'Maybe I could give you advance warning to get a few books moved beforehand. It is books you're into, isn't it?'

'Books and knowledge are my life,' said Drusilla, drawing herself up. 'I won't let you sweep it aside for – for what? Why are you even doing this?'

'The rivers are in my blood,' said Jordan Shore. 'I'm not sure the saying that blood is thicker than water applies to me.' He swept a hand round the office. 'Beneath all this is the river, and soon I'll set it free. Water, water everywhere.' His eyes gleamed with a pale watery light, like the reflection of the moon in a puddle. 'River Logistics, led by me, will set up new networks and infrastructure to cope with a changing landscape. That's what people will need, and what they'll pay for.' His eyes gleamed.

'That's more than you said in the *Financial Times*,' said Jemma.

'It doesn't do to be too candid in public,' the CEO replied, and Jemma hoped beyond hope that her phone had connected to Sergeant Hawkins and wouldn't run out of battery. Apart from anything else, the telltale beep would probably finish her off.

Drusilla lifted her chin. 'I refuse,' she said. 'I take back my offer. I won't be party to this – this destruction.' Jemma thought of the book she had captured in the British Library, and her mouth twitched.

'That's a shame, Drusilla,' said Jordan Shore, showing no emotion whatsoever. He pointed a finger at Jemma. 'You stay there.' Immediately, Jemma felt as if her feet were welded to the floor. 'You and I, Ms James, have unfinished business.' He swivelled to face Drusilla. 'I loaned you certain powers and privileges based on your promises to me. As you have chosen not to fulfil those promises, I'm taking them back.'

'Please—' said Drusilla, starting forward, but she was too late. Jordan Shore pinched his thumb and forefinger together as if grasping a thread, and pulled it towards him. 'Aaahh!' Drusilla's head snapped back, and her chest jerked forward as if he had pulled her heart out. At lightning speed she shrivelled to half her size, wrinkling like a walnut, and collapsed on the floor.

'What have you done?' cried Jemma. 'Raphael, do something!' She bent down and tried to move her legs, but they wouldn't budge.

Raphael crossed the room and gently lifted Drusilla's head. 'There isn't much I can do,' he said. 'She isn't dead, but she's close to it.'

'Help me,' Drusilla croaked. 'Don't let him near me. Or her.' She had just enough strength left to glare at Jemma.

'Lennox, is there anything you can do?' asked Raphael.

Lennox gave the CEO a nervous glance. 'Sorry, no,' he said.

'I can finish her off now, if you like,' said Jordan Shore. 'It wouldn't take long.'

'Shut up,' said Jemma. She turned to Drusilla, who was curled in a ball, trembling. *What can I do? I can't help . . . or can I?* 'Drusilla, what was the last book you read?'

Drusilla's eyes found her, but their bright hazel had faded to pale, milky brown. 'The last book I read?' A long pause. 'It's been a while.'

Yes, because you've been too busy causing trouble, thought Jemma. 'Tell me about your favourite book, then,' she said.

'My favourite book?' Drusilla's tongue ran over her wrinkled lips. 'When I was a girl, my mother had a subscription to the circulating library. She brought back the first volume of a book called *Jane Eyre*. I don't know if you've heard of that.'

'Yes, I have,' said Jemma, fighting the urge to snap at her.

'She wouldn't let me read it – it was too grown-up for me, she said – but I sneaked down from the nursery when I was meant to be asleep, and read by the light of the dying fire. I finished it well before she did, and had to wait for her to bring home the second volume, then the third. It was the first time I really lost myself in a book.' Drusilla's mouth curled at the edges like an old parchment. 'Later, of course, I learned that novels were silly and vulgar and one should not waste one's time on them.' She sighed. 'I had forgotten all that.'

'Perhaps you can read it again some day,' said Jemma, blinking back a tear.

'I don't know why you're wasting your time chatting to an old crone when you could be making a deal with me,' said Jordan Shore. 'This isn't a ruddy book club.'

'A book club would be much better,' Jemma retorted. She heard a tiny creak outside, and her heart leapt. Then it sank. What could anyone do against Jordan Shore? The person lurking was probably a member of staff, anyway. But if it was someone who could help... She studied Jordan Shore. 'Maybe I will make a deal with you.'

'Jemma, no!' cried Raphael.

Jemma grinned. 'When hell freezes over.'

Jordan Shore's eyes narrowed and he sat up straight. 'You're feisty now, Jemma James,' he said, 'but you'll change your tune once we've spent more time together—'

The door flew open and police officers spilled into the room, pointing guns at everyone. Then another officer walked in, and under the cap Jemma saw the dark, beady eyes of Sergeant Hawkins. He scanned the room. 'Right, you lot, your guns should be pointing at that chap.' He pointed at Lennox, who had flung his hands up.

'Why me?' he cried. 'What about everyone else? What about him?' He jerked his head towards Jordan Shore.

'I'm dealing with him,' said Sergeant Hawkins. He walked forward until he was standing in front of the desk. 'Jemma, you can end the call. We've got enough.'

Jordan Shore sprang to his feet, glaring at Jemma, but Sergeant Hawkins raised his hand and moved it sharply forward. Jordan Shore slammed into his chair, which shot backwards and hit the wall. 'I told you to pack it in,' said Sergeant Hawkins. 'I suggest you listen. In fact—' He mimed pulling a zipper across his mouth. The CEO's eyes bulged and he moved his head convulsively from side to side, but that was all he could do. 'Just while I deal with this,' said Sergeant Hawkins. He took out a notebook and pencil. 'So, present we have Jordan Shore, Jemma James – of course – Raphael Burns…'

'Good to see you, Mike,' said Raphael. 'It's been a while.'

Sergeant Hawkins gave him a stern look. 'Likewise, Raph, but it's Sergeant Hawkins when I'm on duty.'

Jemma was taking this in, and storing it up for later discussion, when she heard a scraping sound coming from the floor. Drusilla was creeping towards her with agonising slowness. The sight of her made Jemma's skin crawl. 'Stop that,' she said.

'I won't hurt you,' wheezed Drusilla.

'What's going on there?' said Sergeant Hawkins.

'Jordan Shore stuck me to the floor,' said Jemma. 'And I think Drusilla is planning to bite my ankle.'

'Oh, for heaven's sake.' Sergeant Hawkins clicked his fingers and the heaviness left Jemma's legs. 'It's never straightforward, is it?' He turned to Lennox. 'I suppose you're the worthy Dr Lennox Nash. I've heard a great deal about you.'

Lennox smiled weakly, his hands still in the air. 'All

good, I hope.'

The sergeant regarded him for some time before answering. 'If that's what you want to believe, go right ahead.' He went to Raphael, and they conversed in low tones.

Drusilla was still inching her way towards Jemma, who crouched down in exasperation. 'What are you doing?' she muttered.

'I'm sorry,' said Drusilla.

'Good,' Jemma replied. 'You should be. And people think *I* make a mess.'

'It got out of hand,' Drusilla whispered. 'If they arrest me, they'll keep me alive like this. For the trial and my sentence, which will be a long one. Stay where you are, and you can help me.'

'I can't help you,' said Jemma. 'Lennox sacked me from my job and the Keepers' Guild, and you made me take off my bracelet. There's nothing I can do.'

Sergeant Hawkins looked around. 'I'm glad you two are having a nice chat, but I'm trying to work here.'

Jemma stood up and beckoned him over. 'Will you keep her alive? Will you really make her stand trial, and serve her sentence, like this?'

His face could have been carved from stone. 'That's the official protocol, yes.' He returned to Raphael, his back to Jemma. 'Officers, move forward,' he said. 'Watch these two closely.'

The police officers obediently shuffled forward until they surrounded the CEO's desk, focusing on him and Lennox.

Jemma crouched beside Drusilla. 'What do you want me to do?' she murmured.

Drusilla mouthed something so faint that Jemma couldn't hear her. She tried again. 'Hold out your hand.'

Jemma shrugged and did as she asked. 'It won't do anything.'

Drusilla wheezed, and eventually Jemma realised it was supposed to be a laugh. 'Maybe you'll surprise yourself.' Her voice was like dry leaves. 'And maybe I should have listened to you. Too late now.' She inched herself forward once more and reached out to Jemma. 'Goodbye,' she said. And as her hand touched Jemma's, she crumbled into pale-grey ash.

Chapter 21

'So it ended as well as it could, really,' said Jemma. 'I don't know what will happen with River Logistics, but I'll tell you when I do.'

Water lapped against the stone steps as the octopus stretched out a tentacle. Jemma patted it. 'See you soon.' She picked up the lantern, waved, and ascended to the trapdoor as with a splash, the octopus vanished beneath the surface. Then she replaced the floor coverings, extinguished the lantern, and went downstairs.

'All in order?' asked Raphael. He was sitting in one of the armchairs near the café area, a black coffee and a Danish pastry at his elbow, surveying the scene in a pleased manner.

'Yes, everything's fine in there,' said Jemma. 'As far as I can tell.' Though Raphael had reinstated her membership of the Keepers' Guild, she was still uncertain whether her powers were at their former strength or not. She glanced at her left wrist, which was still bare, but it wasn't the right time to discuss such things. 'Are you enjoying your return to Burns Books?'

'I am,' said Raphael. 'A few things are different, and I miss having Folio about all the time, but while Italy was lovely, it was only ever temporary. Giulia and I both knew that. It's just a shame I had to rush back so quickly.'

Jemma plumped herself down in the armchair beside his. 'I didn't realise you were on your way home when I texted you. I thought you were ignoring me.'

Raphael looked across at her. 'I'm sorry. At least everything is fixed now.'

'Yes,' said Jemma. 'I suppose it is.'

In the basement of River Logistics, Raphael had gently moved her away from the small pile of ash that had once been Drusilla Davenport. 'I'm so sorry,' he said. 'I didn't see what was happening. Let's get you out of here. Mike and the police can deal with the rest of it.'

He muttered something to Sergeant Hawkins, then supported Jemma along the corridor and into the lift. 'And I'm sorry I ambushed you outside the building. I presumed you were trying to get in, and I figured it was the best way to get us both in and find out as much as we could.'

'Well, it worked,' said Jemma. 'Thinking back, I should have spotted you, but I was in shock. Anyway, it's done now.'

'Yes. It's done now.'

The lift door opened into the foyer and they saw first more police officers, spread liberally around the area, and then, sitting on an uncomfortable-looking black leather and steel sofa, Luke, Maddy, Em, and Carl. The moment they saw Jemma and Raphael, they leapt to their feet and charged over. Carl enveloped Jemma in an enormous hug, and the others crowded round, adding to the hug, until they resembled a many-legged monster.

Luke was the first to turn to Raphael. 'How did you get here?' he demanded. 'I never saw you go in. Were you here already?'

'In a manner of speaking,' said Raphael, with a wry smile. 'I, er, assisted Jemma into the building.'

'No you didn't,' said Luke. 'I saw everything. There was a bloke with a guidebook who morphed into Drusilla, and— Oh!' He stared at Raphael, his eyes as round as green glass marbles.

'Yes,' said Raphael. 'I'm rather tired.' He went to the nearest chair and sat down heavily.

'Let's all sit down,' said Jemma. 'Everything is being dealt with. We can rest. In fact—' She turned to the nearest police officer. 'Would you mind if we went and got a cup of coffee? It's been quite an afternoon.'

'I daresay it has, madam,' he said, stiffly. 'And yes, providing you leave your details and a contact number, I don't see a problem with that. Sarge is busy downstairs; I doubt he'll get to you today.'

Thank heavens for that. While she was tremendously grateful that Sergeant Hawkins had managed to reach them in time, the notion of giving a statement, watched by those dark, beady eyes, made her knees wobble. More so, now she knew what Sergeant Hawkins was capable of.

They had caught a couple of taxis to Burns Books, opened up, and Em and Carl had dispensed as much caffeine and as many snacks as anyone could want.

'What happened, Jemma?' asked Maddy. 'I mean, obviously everything's fine now, but what was Lennox doing there? And who was behind it? Was it the CEO guy?'

Jemma studied Maddy's enquiring face and wondered how on earth to answer. *How can I explain what I went through in there?* She imagined describing the moment when Drusilla had touched her, and shivered. 'I will tell you,' she said, 'but not yet. At the moment, to be honest, I want to focus on the future.' She looked down at herself. 'And change out of these clothes. I don't feel like myself.'

'I know what you mean,' said Maddy. She had removed her blonde wig, but the stripy top and jeans remained. 'It's much too . . . not-black.'

'Speaking of the future,' said Luke, taking Maddy's hand, 'Maddy and I have got something to tell you. We're, um, taking our relationship to a new level.'

Jemma clapped her hand to her mouth. 'No, Maddy, you can't! Not after all this!' She inspected Maddy's neck frantically for bites before realising that Maddy was holding out her left hand, and on her finger was a silver ring set with a stone so black that it seemed to absorb light. 'Oh!' She dived forward and wrapped Maddy in a hug. 'I'm so glad!' *And so relieved.*

'Yes, we're engaged,' said Luke drily. 'Not the other thing. That's why I sneaked Maddy into our own taxi, to propose. And no, we haven't set a date yet. But we want you all to come and be bridesmaids and ushers and stuff like that.'

At that point, Raphael had excused himself and

returned with a bottle of champagne, and they had toasted the happy couple with fizz in teacups. *I'm glad something nice has come out of this. It's been a heck of a journey, though.*

She thought it again now as she looked at Raphael. Around them, the shop was busy. Em was dealing with a queue at the café counter, while Luke was chatting with the Golden Age crime ladies and ringing up their books.

Ben, meanwhile, was in charge of the till upstairs. Raphael had been dismayed at his appointment, but concluded after a period of observation that he was mostly harmless. 'He may stay,' he had said. 'We need an extra pair of hands.' Ben seemed willing, and even reasonably diligent. Jemma found it strange that he never asked where Lennox had gone, but decided, after some thought, that Lennox's bad influence, and Ben's memory of him, had faded once Em's glamour replaced Lennox's.

'Why do we need an extra pair of hands?' she asked, narrowing her eyes at Raphael. 'I mean, you're back.'

'That is true,' said Raphael. 'In response, I shall now answer the million-dollar question.'

'Excuse me?'

'The one you've been asking me for what feels like millennia. About what I was doing in Italy.'

Jemma heard an emphatic throat-clearing behind her, and twisted round to find Em holding a large cappuccino. She beamed at her. 'You're a mind reader,' she said, taking the cup.

'Not exactly,' said Em. 'But in your case, it's hardly difficult.' She glanced at Raphael. 'I'll leave you to get on.

Things to do, people to, um, see.' She had a determined look on her face.

'I wonder what that's about,' said Jemma, watching Em walk back to the café. 'Anyway. Yes, Italy.'

'Quite,' said Raphael. 'This is what I asked you over for, really. The stockroom was a decoy.'

Jemma's eyebrows shot up. *I don't think I can cope with more changes.*

'I haven't been entirely truthful with you, Jemma,' said Raphael.

'OK...' Jemma concentrated on keeping her expression interested rather than aghast. *What is it? What on earth is it?*

'While I *was* exhausted by that little run-in at Drusilla's place, and I *did* need a rest, my objective in talking to Armand Dupont was more extensive than I had you believe. I have been dealing with various small administrative matters in Italy, but my main focus was on succession planning.'

Jemma's jaw dropped. 'Succession planning?'

'That's what I said,' said Raphael. 'One of my main reasons for going away was to ascertain how you would manage without me. After you turned down the offer to deputise as Keeper, Lennox Nash was never intended as a serious replacement. I wanted to know how long it would take you to see through him and take on matters yourself.'

Jemma could do nothing but goggle at him. 'You – you —'

'So I was often unavailable,' said Raphael. 'Armand and I were monitoring the situation, of course. If things had got really bad we would have stepped in – though I didn't expect such infamy from Lennox, and neither did I expect things to escalate so quickly.' He finished his coffee and put the cup down. 'That is why it's time for me to step aside. While I still have my uses, I'm getting too old for this game.'

'You can't leave,' said Jemma. 'You've only just come back.'

Raphael laughed. 'I have no intention of leaving, and Giulia was pining for Rolando's. What Armand has suggested is that I become Keeper Emeritus. An advisor, rather than an actor. So I'll have more time for book-buying trips. Which reminds me, I must take Gertrude for a spin.' He raised an eyebrow. 'Fancy a trip to Elinor Dashwood's?'

'Yes, of course,' said Jemma. 'Don't sidetrack.'

Raphael sighed, with a sly look at her. 'While we've put paid to Jordan Shore's antics for now, I suspect there will be many more attempted coups and civil wars in the future. We need more staff not fewer, a less hierarchical structure, a board at the top instead of one person, and someone dedicated to guide that board. And yes, Jemma, I mean you.'

'Me?' Jemma felt utterly bewildered. 'I'm not even sure I have Assistant Keeper powers any more.'

'Drusilla wouldn't go near you until she had to,' said Raphael. 'She knew how powerful you are.'

'That was the bracelet. That was the only way I could get past Lennox—'

'No, it wasn't,' said Raphael. 'The bracelet was another

little trick of mine, I'm afraid. The beads on it are semi-precious stones, and it confers no power whatsoever. The one thing it does do is track your whereabouts when asked, which was handy when I wanted to meet you outside River Logistics.' He laughed as Jemma opened and shut her mouth like a fish. 'The things you did were all you.'

Raphael looked around the shop; everyone was busy. He pointed at the crime shelves, beckoned with one finger, and a copy of *Crooked House* shot into his hand. 'Now you have a go.'

Jemma concentrated hard on the shelves, pointed, then beckoned. 'Aargh!' she cried, and flung up her arms to protect herself as several books made a beeline for her.

'See?' said Raphael. 'You just need to control it better. I suggested the title Keeper at Large to Armand and he rather liked it. Plus with the way Luke, Em and Maddy are coming on, you'll have great backup. Have a chat with Carl, why don't you, and sleep on it.' He smiled at her. 'No pressure, but I've arranged a chat for us three tomorrow morning to go through the details.' He examined the book he was holding. 'Haven't read this in ages,' he said, and opened it.

Jemma drank her cappuccino, said a quick goodbye to Luke and Em, then set off upstairs. Someone was standing at the top, fidgeting, and as she drew nearer she realised it was Damon. He was wearing a raincoat over jeans and a T-shirt, and his shoes didn't match. He looked utterly bewildered.

'Where is she?' he demanded. 'Where's Em? I don't know how I got here, but I have to see her.'

'She's downstairs in the café,' said Jemma, and stood aside as he clattered past.

'Em!' he cried. 'I'm coming!'

Shaking her head, Jemma waved to Ben as she walked out.

As she strolled to the Friendly Bookshop, her phone – her usual phone – buzzed. A text from Jasper: *Would you like to have lunch with me? We could meet at the hotel. We have so much to say to each other.*

Jemma smiled, and moved into a doorway to reply. *I'm busy in the shop today, but definitely another time.* She paused, considering what else to add, then shook her head and pressed *Send*. Everything else she wanted to say could be said in person. Once she'd decided what that was.

***

'Oh, there you are,' said Maddy, as Jemma came in. 'Carl offered to mind the till over lunch, but I thought I'd better wait for you.'

A magazine was open on the counter. Jemma read the upside-down headline: *Your Dream Gothic Wedding. I dread to think what the bridesmaids' dresses will be like.* 'See you in an hour,' she said, as Maddy closed the magazine and picked up her bag.

She went into the back room, where Carl was frowning at his laptop. 'How's it going?'

'Slowly,' said Carl. 'Stop wriggling, you lot,' he said, looking down.

Jemma came closer and saw three kittens on his lap. Folio was sitting nearby, watching Carl's progress, and Luna was in her basket washing the tuxedo kitten, who was bearing it quite well. 'I'm not sure they're helping you concentrate,' she said.

'I've thought of names for them, though.'

'Have you?'

'Yes. Isis for the black one, Jinx for the ginger one, Cleo for the tortoiseshell one, and Frankie for Mr Mucky there,' he said, indicating the tuxedo kitten.

Jemma inspected the kittens, considering. 'You know what,' she said, 'I think you've got it.' She stroked each kitten and said their names, and the kittens squeaked in reply. 'It's official.' She grinned at him. 'There you are, you've achieved something.'

'That's more than I'm doing with this,' Carl replied, closing the laptop. 'I should bin it and start again. It's meant to be edgy but it's just meh, and I said I'd have a full draft for Michael and Janina when I got back.' He glanced at Jemma. 'What I really want to do is write about the bookshop, but I can't.'

Jemma sat opposite him and took his hand. 'Maybe you can. Not directly, but no one can stop you writing about a magical bookshop, can they? All bookshops are magical in their own way.'

'*The Magical Bookshop*,' said Carl, placing the words in the air in front of him. 'I'd buy tickets for a play called that, wouldn't you?' His eyes were bright as he reopened the laptop. Even the kittens had stopped wriggling.

Jemma smiled. 'I'll leave you to it. I'm meeting Hermione for coffee at two, but Maddy will be back by then.' She kissed the top of his head, stroked each of the cats, and went through to the main shop. There she sat down at the counter and thought of all the things she ought to be doing – inspecting the stockroom, making a list of books to buy when she and Raphael visited Elinor Dashwood, planning the Easter window display – but her head was too full of other things. Then her question to Drusilla came into her head: *What was the last book you read?*

'I'm not sure,' she said aloud. 'It seems ages since I curled up with a book.'

On impulse, she got up and went to the shelves. She saw many books she had read, and some she didn't think she'd enjoy. Then she remembered the first time she had met Raphael, when she had chosen a book to put him in his place. Not that it had, of course. *Anna Karenina, and I never did open it.* She snorted, then went to the shelves to see if they had a copy. They did.

Her hand hovered over the book. *I might not like it.*

But you won't know unless you begin. She pulled out the book and took it to the counter.

A soft black cloud on a flurry of legs arrived with a skittering of claws, and resolved itself into Luna. She rubbed her cheek against the book. 'I see you approve,' said Jemma. Folio jumped up beside Luna, nuzzled her, and settled in the light of a sunbeam which turned his tawny fur to gold.

She heard a squeak from the floor, and looked down. The tuxedo kitten, Frankie, was gazing at her with huge green eyes. *I'm sure his eyes were blue before.* She sighed. 'OK,' she said, lifting him onto her lap, 'but you must promise to be good. No wriggling, and no squeaking.'

'Meep,' said Frankie, and sneezed. The force of it sent him a few feet into the air, but he floated down to Jemma's lap like a falling leaf.

Jemma stared at the kitten with eyes as round as his own. 'Good heavens.'

'Meep,' Frankie agreed, and curled himself into a ball.

Magical kittens. I wasn't prepared for that.

'Now, who are the main characters?' murmured Carl, in the back room.

Jemma smiled, opened her book, and began reading.

What to Read Next

Fully Booked marks the end of the Magical Bookshop series arc, but that isn't necessarily the last you'll see of these characters. I'm actually in the process of editing a new book featuring many of them, and I'm hoping that will become a new series of its own. If you either follow me on Amazon or sign up for my newsletter (via my website), you'll know when it comes out!

Until then, here are a few other books to take a look at.

If you've enjoyed the cozy fantasy and magic of this series, you might like the Lulmouth Bay fantasy romcom series I'm writing with Paula Harmon. The first book in the series is *A Tale of Tea and Dragons* – and there's a mystery element too.

Welcome to Lulmouth Bay, a seaside town with a difference…

Enchanter Hannah brews magical teas which make the tearoom she inherited a success. Yet she's trapped in her grandmother's vision, and longs to be more than friends with the man she's loved since school.

Tea and spice merchant Max has learnt to hide his powers, coming from a place where magic is a forbidden secret. And after a failed romance with a fellow Enchanter, he's only looking for fun.

It's dislike at first sight, but the stakes are high…

Check the book out here: http://mybook.to/LBay1

If you like the supernatural element of the mystery, you might enjoy my Spirit of the Law series. The first book in the series is *The Case of the Four Fingers*.

Meet a detective duo – a century apart!

When new constable Steph is sent to mark time at a Liverpool police station on the verge of closing, she sees it as the death of her career. Then she meets Nora, the hundred-year-old ghost of a police officer, who's determined to get a few more cases under her belt.

Together they investigate the Case of the Four Fingers, a macabre episode which has haunted Nora for over sixty years.

See the book here: http://mybook.to/Fingers

Acknowledgements

Thanks to my excellent beta-readers – Carol Bissett, Ruth Cunliffe, Paula Harmon, and Stephen Lenhardt – for putting up with possibly even more nonsense than usual (and no, I didn't warn them about the octopus!), and my equally long-suffering and wonderful proofreader, John Croall.

I must add extra thanks to my husband Stephen Lenhardt for additional moral support, and especially for sympathising when I'm moaning that I've been rained on, hailed on, or occasionally snowed on during a drafting walk. Let's face it, what else would happen in January?

If you're interested in visiting or learning more about the places Jemma visits, here are some resources:

London Mithraeum: https://www.londonmithraeum.com

St Stephen Walbrook: https://ststephenwalbrook.net

The London Stone: https://www.museumoflondon.org.uk/discover/london-stone-seven-strange-myths

As usual, while I've tried to make places like the London Library and the Maughan Library resemble their real-world counterparts, the staff I've depicted there are entirely imaginary. Likewise, River Logistics isn't based on any real-life courier firms!

And as always, my final thanks go to you, the reader. I hope you've enjoyed the latest adventure of Jemma and her accomplices. I won't say last, as some characters have more to say – and also because I've learned never to say never as it will come back to bite me! However, this story arc is complete.

I've had a wonderful time writing this series, which sprang out of a desire to write the sort of light, comforting book that I wanted to read during lockdown. Thank you for coming on the journey with me!

If you'd like to get in touch, or stay in contact, do send me a message via my website, or sign up for my newsletter.

If you have enjoyed this book, a short review or a rating on Amazon or Goodreads would be very much appreciated. Ratings and reviews, however short, help readers to discover books.

FONT AND IMAGE CREDITS

Cover and heading fonts: Alyssum Blossom and Alyssum Blossom Sans by Bombastype.

Cats (eye colour changed in some instances): Vector cats set. animal pet, wildcat and kitten, hunter and predator, black silhouette illustration Free Vector by macrovector at freepik.com: https://www.freepik.com/free-vector/vector-cats-set-animal-pet-wildcat-kitten-hunter-predator-black-silhouette-illustration_10704168.htm

Sea (cropped and recoloured): Sea waves vector seamless abstract hand-drawn pattern for wallpaper Free Vector by macrovector at freepik.com: https://www.freepik.com/free-vector/sea-waves-vector-seamless-abstract-hand-drawn-pattern-wallpaper_10603879.htm

Books: Vintage book elements collection with different books Free Vector by macrovector: https://www.freepik.com/free-vector/vintage-book-elements-collection-with-different-books_9397979.htm

Stars: Night free icon by flaticon at freepik.com: https://www.freepik.com/free-icon/night_914336.htm

Cover created using GIMP image editor: https://www.gimp.org

About the Author

Liz Hedgecock grew up in London, England, did an English degree, and then took forever to start writing. After several years working in the National Health Service, some short stories crept into the world. A few even won prizes. Then the stories started to grow longer…

Now Liz travels between the nineteenth and twenty-first centuries, murdering people. To be fair, she does usually clean up after herself.

Liz's reimaginings of Sherlock Holmes, her Pippa Parker cozy mystery series, the Caster & Fleet Victorian mystery series (written with Paula Harmon), the Magical Bookshop series, and the Maisie Frobisher Mysteries are available in ebook and paperback.

Liz lives in Cheshire with her husband and two sons, and when she's not writing or child-wrangling you can usually find her reading, messing about on Twitter, or cooing over stuff in museums and art galleries. That's her story, anyway, and she's sticking to it.

Website/blog: http://lizhedgecock.wordpress.com
Facebook: http://www.facebook.com/lizhedgecockwrites
Twitter: http://twitter.com/lizhedgecock
Goodreads: https://www.goodreads.com/lizhedgecock

Books by Liz Hedgecock

To check out any of my books, please visit my Amazon author page at http://author.to/LizH. If you follow me there, you'll be notified whenever I release a new book.

Lulmouth Bay (1 novel: book 2 coming soon)
Welcome to Lulmouth Bay, a seaside town with a difference. It's a magical town where imps, elves and merpeople mix with normal folk and romance may be just around the corner…

The Magical Bookshop (6 novels)
An eccentric owner, a hostile cat, and a bookshop with a mind of its own. Can Jemma turn around the second-worst secondhand bookshop in London? And can she learn its secrets?

Booker & Fitch Mysteries (6 novels, with Paula Harmon)
Jade Fitch hopes for a fresh start when she opens a new-age shop in a picturesque market town. Meanwhile, Fi Booker runs a floating bookshop as well as dealing with her teenage son. And as soon as they meet, it's murder…

Caster & Fleet Mysteries (6 novels, with Paula Harmon)
There's a new detective duo in Victorian London . . . and they're women! Meet Katherine and Connie, two young women who become partners in crime. Solving it, that is!

Maisie Frobisher Mysteries (6 novels)
When Maisie Frobisher, a bored young Victorian socialite, goes travelling in search of adventure, she finds more than she could ever have dreamt of. Mystery, intrigue and a touch of romance.

Mrs Hudson & Sherlock Holmes (3 novels)
Mrs Hudson is Sherlock Holmes's elderly landlady. Or is she? Find out her real story here.

Pippa Parker Mysteries (6 novels)
Meet Pippa Parker: mum, amateur sleuth, and resident of a quaint English village called Much Gadding. And then the murders began...

The Spirit of the Law (3 novellas)
Meet a detective duo – a century apart! A modern-day police constable and a hundred-year-old ghost team up to solve the coldest of cases.

Sherlock & Jack (3 novellas)
Jack has been ducking and diving all her life. But when she meets the great detective Sherlock Holmes they form an unlikely partnership. And Jack discovers that she is more important than she ever realised...

Tales of Meadley (3 novelettes)
A romantic comedy mini-series based in the village of Meadley, with a touch of mystery too.

Halloween Sherlock (3 novelettes)
Short dark tales of Sherlock Holmes and Dr Watson, perfect for a grim winter's night.

For children
A Christmas Carrot (with Zoe Harmon)
Perkins the Halloween Cat (with Lucy Shaw)
Rich Girl, Poor Girl (for 9-12 year olds)

Printed in Dunstable, United Kingdom